WHEN SHADOWS CREEP

WHEN SHADOWS CREEP

By

K. Brooks

ANT COLONY PRESS

Ant Colony Press, a division of Olive Group, LLC,
P.O. Box 1577, Belton, MO 64012

ISBN-13: 978-1-940560-47-2

Ant Colony Press 1st edition January 2018

10 9 8 7 6 5 4 3 2 1

Manufactured in the United States of America

For information regarding special discounts for bulk purchases, please contact Ant Colony Press at antcolonypress@gmail.com.

www.antcolonypress.com

Chapter One

Flynn

As it had for days, the rain pattered against the glass. It drummed a rhythm behind the rivulets that coursed down the window.

Flynn sighed and settled his mug down onto the sill. The steam from his cup spiraled up and condensed against the glass, and he drew his finger across the fog. He divided the round cloud and left the droplet of moisture to hover on his fingertip.

A car door slammed and startled him from where he stared at the horizon and drew his eyes down to the curb.

"Caden," he hissed; the exhalation clouded his vision. He palmed the glass, smearing the sight of the man who stared up from the muddy lawn below. The brilliant red jacket of his unwanted visitor glowed. The color unnatural against the dead leaves and rotten grass.

The figure waved.

He backed away from the window into the storm-darkened room. He settled down into the worn armchair that bumped against his calves. He drummed his fingers against the threadbare arm of the chair. The thumb of his other hand circled a cigarette burn in the gray-green fabric.

"He shouldn't be here. Shouldn't, shouldn't," he muttered, silenced as the doorbell rang.

He held his breath.

Maybe he will just leave.

The doorbell pealed once more.

Damn.

The hand that agitated the fabric of the chair stopped. It moved to the bridge of his nose and pinched the cartilage between furrowed brows.

A rusted hinge squealed from two floors below. Footsteps sounded a slow, measured pace that knocked on the bare wooden stairs.

"Flynn…" The voice called from the stairwell, dragged out the end of his name in a juvenile taunt.

The raised hood came first, an aggressive red against the drab plaster background. Caden dragged his fingertips along the walls as he approached. It was an unpleasant, whispered sound that ground in Flynn's ears. The doorway filled with Caden's hulking shape. The hood of his ruby jacket shaded his face and the sleeves hid his hands, along with anything he may have carried.

When Shadows Creep

Caden had to duck to enter the room, though the peak of his hood still knocked against the sill. It settled around his shoulders.

"Dramatic," Flynn observed as he attempted to hide that he chewed on the inside of his cheek.

Caden shrugged as his eyes darted around the room, took in the shabby surroundings. "As dramatic as refusing to answer the door, Flynn."

Flynn rolled his eyes, settled more firmly into the armchair. "You're under the impression that I want you here," Flynn glowered.

Caden issued a hoarse, barking laugh and strode further into the room. There was a moment's hesitation as he looked between his seating options of the mismatched furniture strewn about the room. He grabbed a wooden ladder back chair and dragged it over in front of Flynn. He straddled backward on the seat and rested his large hands on the back rungs. He eyed Flynn as he waited.

A few beats ticked by. Caden cleared his throat, "Maybe not want. But need. For sure,"

Flynn steepled his fingers, glared over the tips.

"I know you're trying to set me on fire with your thoughts, Flynn. But it hasn't worked once in the past thirty years, why would it work now?"

"Persistence."

It was Caden's turn, and he rolled his eyes. He brushed the water droplets from his hair. It confirmed what Flynn had suspected. The hood was for a dramatic presentation. He'd only donned it upon his entry to the house.

The staccato of rain thundered loud against the roof and the window, as the frigid rain turned to hail. Flynn shivered.

"Look, you can't stay here anymore, not alone," Caden held out his hands, gestured at the room.

Flynn stared at him.

A low, slow rumble of thunder dragged its way across the sky.

"Nothing you say will make me leave. There's nothing out there for me. I'm fine here. I swear, always have been, and always will be."

"I don't think you quite understand the circumstances, Flynn, things have changed."

"I understand enough." Flynn's eyes flicked to the shadowed corner of the attic room.

Caden followed Flynn's gaze, stared a moment before he turned back to study Flynn's face. "Then why aren't you terrified? You should have been far away from here, as soon as you found out."

Flynn shrugged once more. "I don't bother them, they don't bother me. What's the problem?"

Caden tutted under his breath, shook his head.

The air had cooled, foggy plumes streamed from their mouths as they exhaled. Flynn rubbed his hands together,

When Shadows Creep

willed the heat to turn back on. The furnace had been spotty at best, had a hard time reaching the uppermost room of this old house.

"It's not the furnace, Flynn, you know that."

"Don't bring attention to it."

"Flynn, please. Come with me, we can protect you."

"Caden, stop it," Flynn spat.

"You're leaving here, one way or another. Don't make me do this, don't make me come back here." Caden stood, rising to his full height. He stared down at the man curled against the worn out upholstery as if it offered protection.

"You're worse than they are, you're a bully."

Caden cocked his head to the side in response and winced. He pinched the bridge of his nose and sighed.

"Really Flynn? Me? Worse than these, what, harbingers? Really? Them?!" Caden turned and gestured at the shadows, the pressure of dark around the edges of the room. The darkness shifted for a moment, the room brightened despite the pouring rain.

The effect collapsed after a few heartbeats, the room darker than before.

Flynn smiled regretfully. The shadows that had been watching the argument below had tried to reassure Caden. Flynn knew exactly what would come next.

Flynn rubbed at his forehead. "Now look, you've upset it."

Chapter Two

Carmen

Carmen was concerned.

Caden had left hours ago, had checked in when he reached halfway, and hadn't been heard from since.

The roads had been slick for days from the ever-present mist freezing and thawing and freezing again. The rest of the time rain thundered down in a deluge or hammered the earth with hail the size of quarters. It was all too easy to imagine Caden had wrecked the car, spun out and rolled over in a flooded ditch.

Carmen shuddered.

"Wicked weather. Wicked to hide wicked deeds," a voice chided from somewhere behind Carmen's back.

Carmen turned to look at the newcomer.

"You would know, Finnigan."

A strange noise issued from Finnigan's mouth, half laugh, half sigh. He joined Carmen at the window and gazed out into the depths of the night. The wind had picked up

When Shadows Creep

in the last half hour. It whispered around the corners and through the crevices of the upper stories of the old house. Out here, there was no glow of cities, no streetlights to gild the edges of the heavy storm clouds.

Finnigan turned from the heavy storm clouds outside and took a seat next to the fire. He rested his boots against the warm stone below the mantle and snuggled down into the overstuffed chair. He ran a finger around the crystal rim of Carmen's abandoned whiskey. He made the glass sing, plaintive against the storm.

"You worry too much, Carm."

"I worry precisely as much as I need to, Finnigan."

"Which in this case, is none at all. So relax. He'll return, Flynn in tow, and nothing more will come of this absurdity."

"This *absurdity* is that your brother has been cursed. *This* is a disaster," Carmen turned away from the window and rested against the sill, arms crossed.

Finnigan shrugged from his seat.

Carmen stared at the back of Finnigan's chair for a moment, then continued. "It's the company he keeps. Or lack thereof. They've preyed on him. And they won't let him be unless we all do something about it."

Finnigan yawned, loud in the silence, and stretched in his seat. He raised his chin and turned his head to look at Carmen from the corner of his eye. "You do something about it. I'm done with him. I was done with him years ago."

Carmen lost patience, strode across the room, and cuffed Finnigan across the back of the head. "That's *precisely the problem*, Finnigan!"

"Easy!" Finnigan barked.

Carmen plopped down into the chair across from Finnigan, shook a finger in his direction. "None of this will be fixed if you ignore Flynn. I won't let you relegate him to some, some *bottom feeder* unworthy of your time while he's here, alright? You will be a help, Finnigan, or you will leave, I will make sure of it."

Finnigan rolled his eyes and crossed his arms, sinking ever lower into the chair.

Carmen glared at him and thought of all the ways to knock that pout off of Finnigan's face.

Finnigan sat silent for a moment then asked, "Who died and made you house leader, huh? What's Roman got to say about all this?"

"You know well that Roman hasn't been here in a week. Someone had to step up."

"What?" Finnigan sat up straight, hands clenched between his knees, lines etched across his forehead.

"Oh quit making that face, Finnigan. I know you know," Carmen waved a hand in his direction and settled back into the chair.

Finnigan shook his head, mouth agape. "Where did he go? Where could he go? He has to. He is. He couldn't?"

When Shadows Creep

Carmen waited for Finnigan to generate complete sentences, but it never happened.

"Just another reason why I sent Caden to retrieve Flynn. It will be safer for us in the event Roman's return is delayed."

Finnigan rubbed his mouth with his hand. He stared at his other hand with an incredulous expression.

The clock on the mantle ticked several loud beats by. A crack of lightning disturbed the quiet, chased by a rumble of thunder.

"It will all be fine, Finnigan. Just trust me. Roman does."

A coy smile played across Finnigan's lips. "Look at me, stealing your job as worrier. It's not a good one."

Carmen settled back, smiled in return. "It's yours now, keep it."

Chapter Three

The Dark

Several years ago...

The Dark had waited. It had watched. It had lived in this house.

It lived in quiet. It wanted nothing more than to cling to the eaves, to observe.

And observe it did.

It saw the comings and goings of the Freemont House. Strangers who would come to the door, seeking refuge from the unending storms.

They never stayed the night. They always chose the cold and wind and rain, the roar of the sea, over the feeling that the Freemont House gave them.

But was *feeling* the best word for it?

Maybe at the core. It was akin to fear, the true explanation far deeper than that. It thrummed down the spine, from the base of the skull to the end of the tail bone. It rattled across the hip bones. It caused goosebumps to rise, skin to twitch.

The never-ending sensation of being watched. The flickers in the corner of their eyes constant.

Something was there.

Something scared them away.

And they would leave. And they would tell their friends. Later, warm, dry, blushed pink across their cheeks. They would wave their drink of choice at a Christmas party, a family dinner, or an office party, perhaps. They would tell the crowd of that time, of that one night that their hand brushed against something darker than themselves. They would recall how they ran as fast and as far as they could into the night. Whatever the weather, whatever the roads, none of it could be as bad as what would happen if they stayed.

Except for him.

He had stayed a night, curled into the mattress, only his coat for warmth, and slept for hours in oblivion.

A sleep so solid in fact, that the storm had washed away unnoticed. The sun rose low and red from the horizon, gilding pink edges along the pale skeletons of the forest trees.

The Dark watched him then, curious.

Could he not feel what they felt? Did their cold and gloom not touch him?

Maybe. Maybe.

The Dark had shrunk back then. Waiting. He would know. He would feel. And then he would leave them. Abandon the Freemont House on its eerie perch above the cliff once more.

But he did not.

He scrubbed the floors and washed the walls.

He removed the sheets from the furniture, washed them and folded them. He put them away in the closet.

He tackled the kitchen, caked and moldy and swollen with moisture and dank.

In time, the inside of the Freemont House returned to a reflection of its former glory.

He trimmed the bushes and cut the grass. He stripped the paint from the grand, wrap-around porch. He replaced it with a vibrant blue that glowed against the dark.

And the Dark marveled.

It marveled as he replaced the bulbs and squinted up into the corners. He tried to figure out why the light, despite the wattage, never seemed to quite fill the room.

He called in cleaners for the duct work. They spent half the day looking over their shoulders, refused to work in the separate rooms alone. He cursed when the attic room remained cold despite the insulation he filled in the walls.

The Dark smiled.

Here, maybe, would be the one.

When Shadows Creep

Flynn

"It doesn't seem to like you much."

Caden slowly sat up from the hardwood floor. He rubbed the back of his head where it had smacked against the scrubbed boards. "Really Flynn? Do ya think?"

Flynn grinned and extended his hand to Caden.

Caden brushed it away and climbed back up to his feet. He put his hands on his hips and stared up at the ceiling. He winced as the angle made his stomach roll. Carmen wouldn't forgive him if Caden came back injured. Too late for that, though.

Flynn flicked imaginary dust from Caden's jacket and gripped him hard by the elbow. "Really, Caden, thank you for visiting. Please, let them all know that I am fine. Everything is in order." Flynn attempted to steer Caden toward the stairs, but it was akin to an attempt to move a large brass statue.

Caden stared down at him. "Last chance, Flynn. Voluntary or no, you'll be joining me."

Flynn's mouth popped open, incredulous. "Sorry that you just got knocked on your ass and lost a few brain cells there. But are you seriously considering forcing me from this home? It isn't necessary. And as you can tell from what literally just happened, they aren't going to let you either!"

Caden placed two immense and heavy hands on Flynn's shoulders and gripped them tight. "Flynn, you have to understand. We're only doing this because we care about you. And Carmen isn't going to let me return unless you're with me, so, please. I want to go home, just please give it a try. If it doesn't work out, I'll personally return you. Back to this. Back to them." Caden's eyes shifted back to the ceiling again.

The tell-tale shadows had left in the wake of their tantrum.

Flynn sank under the weight of Caden's hands, but his voice was steady. "I need you to promise, Caden. I need your word Absolute. The moment I assure Carmen that everything is good, you'll bring me back here."

Caden considered his words, then nodded. "I will agree to this. With a proper Absolute as we must."

The small knife appeared in his hand, dropped from the trigger attached to his wrist. He cut a small x into the ball of his thumb, pulled Flynn's hand tight in his grip, etched his flesh, and pressed their hands together. A faint white light glowed between their hands and faded, little more than a trick of the eyes.

Flynn winced and pulled his hand away. He shook it gently before he inspected the thin white scar left behind.

When Shadows Creep

"I'll soon have to switch hands. I can't tell which one is which anymore."

Caden sighed and began to stride from the room, he shook his head as he went. "Maybe if you ceased making everyone promise, you'd have fewer scars for proof. You can take things a little less to heart, you know,"

Flynn followed Caden down the stairs, his tread a whisper compared to the thud of Caden's step.

"What's the fun in that?"

Caden laughed, the sound loud in the empty hall. They reached the second floor, and Caden gestured at Flynn's room. The bed lamp was lit against the night for when he returned from the attic.

"Will you want to pack? Not sure if Carmen has kept any of your old things?"

Flynn felt small, his place so uncertain in light of these events. Would Carmen have kept anything of his? It was impossible to say. They wanted him with them and that was all he knew. Outside of that…

He gestured down at the pajama pants and holey cardigan that he was wearing. "Likely not the best for travel."

"I'll wait for you downstairs. I am giving you twenty minutes. Gather your things. Say your … *goodbyes?* And then I expect to see you."

Flynn nodded and turned to walk toward the bedroom, and a chill coursed its way down his back.

Caden's voice drifted from where he had descended down the stairs. "Do *not* make me come back up here for you."

. . .

Caden

The wipers streaked the glass at full blast. Despite this, Caden had his nose pressed almost to the windshield as he tried to see where the road turned.

It was hazardous up on the cliffs on a *good* day. The wind always howled whether sunny or stormy and it pushed cars across lines and onto the soft shoulders. The dips and twists and turns were another story. The lows were filled to the brim with dirty rain water, and the highs curved sharply around boulders and trees that sprang from the countryside.

Twice, the road passed through tunnels, the orange lights too bright against their dilated pupils. It made the engine echo and the wheels hum until you shot out into the night once more, blinded.

Flynn was clutching his small bag to his chest. His fingertips and knuckles had gone white against the leather.

"I'm not slowing down, Flynn, not now," Caden growled as he shifted even closer to the windshield.

Flynn gave an imperceptible shake of his head, his eyes fixed on the horizon.

When Shadows Creep

Caden hazarded a glance in his direction and saw his companion had faded to an off-shade of green. He dared to slow the car by several clicks. "I'm sorry, I just... I just wanted to get back as soon as possible," Caden apologized.

Flynn's lips tightened.

"You aren't going to vomit, are you?" Caden gave Flynn another look, and this time waited for his response.

Another head shake.

Caden sighed and eased off the accelerator once more. Flynn's fingers relaxed by a degree.

"I haven't been in a car in years," Flynn said, quiet, no more than a whisper.

"But the house, all that work? How'd you get it all done?"

Flynn wiped at his nose. "You'd be surprised at what the internet can bring you. Wonderful. Truly."

Caden snorted. "But of course. Trust you to have figured all that business out."

The car slowed around a hairpin turn, then rocketed back up to speed on the straightaway.

"*All that business*, Caden? The future is here. The world doesn't need us anymore, it's made its own magic,"

Caden snorted again. He slowed at the approach to a blinking yellow light and stared out into the night for the glimmer of headlights.

"The world is always going to need us, Flynn. That's the way of it, that's what we're here for."

A brief and resigned exhalation came from Flynn, and he turned his gaze away toward the rain-streaked window.

Caden chewed his lip and cleared his throat. "Warm enough?" He fiddled with the dial. The car was a degree below tropical already, but he worried. He worried about the effect that place had on Flynn.

Flynn had put up much more of a fight than he'd expected. Caden believed it was going to take every trick in his repertoire to ensure he never returned to that house.

Chapter Four

Flynn

Flynn stared up at the cold stone walls of Caldwell Manor, amazed that he felt nothing when he gazed upon it. He had expected at the very least to be unsettled. It was a challenge to even muster disdain.

It was squat, inelegant. There were no details, no flourishes, no love lost between these walls. The brick was a dark gray, the roof a dark slate, the windows lightless.

Flynn tilted his head and his gaze roved over the ivy locked in its winter sleep. The land that surrounded the manor had long gone to weeds.

"Can't bother with the mower, Caden? Is it below you?"

Caden ignored him, shouldered past him on the cobblestone path. He headed toward the large wooden front door with its heavy iron knocker.

Flynn turned to glare at Caden's car, parked haphazard across the lawn. He had left it with one tire mashed down over a struggling sapling. "Why do I even ask? He can't even bother to park straight."

A light flicked on from the hall.

Caden's voice called out from behind the half-closed door. "Are you going to come in out of the rain? Or are you going to continue to chastise someone who doesn't care about what you think?"

Flynn's head dropped to his chest and he resumed his trudge towards the mansion. When he got to the door he reached out and rested a hand on the knocker. It was carved in the shape of a hyena head, its mouth snarled around the iron ring shaped as two shooting stars. He paused for a moment. "I know we said goodbye, once. But don't get used to this. I won't be here for long."

He didn't wait for a response. He entered the hall, and his damp clothes began to steam in the warmth as he closed the door behind him.

. . .

Finnigan

"They seem to be here," Finnigan observed.

Carmen nodded, gaze lost in the distance.

"Feel like we should have organized a party," Finnigan lumbered to his feet, numbed by the whiskey and the heat. He trudged toward the door, assumed that Carmen would be on his heels.

When Shadows Creep

But Carmen had not shifted an inch.

"Carmen?" Finnigan frowned, waited. He knocked on the frame. "Hello? Earth to Carmen? We have to go greet Flynn. Are you coming?"

He approached Carmen's chair, rested a hand on a rigid shoulder. No reaction.

A shiver ran down Finnigan's spine.

He swung the chair around on its pivot, which rocked Carmen slightly. Carmen's eyes had rolled back, face stone cold and still. Finnigan sighed, planted a hand on each arm-rest, and leaned forward, until their noses almost touched. "Carm, dear, you'll have to come back from there. Now isn't the time."

Despite the unsettled roll of his stomach, he stared into the whites of Carmen's eyes. He willed them to return to their normal dark hazel.

Several heartbeats thudded by. Finnigan waited.

"Hello?" Caden's voice called from a distance. Finnigan disconnected, straightened away from Carmen's prone form. A sudden gasp, a deep and rough inhalation of air, and Carmen had returned with a shake of the head.

Finnigan crossed his arms, lips pursed. "You could warn me next time you go on a stroll, Carm."

Carmen blinked, looked around and scrambled up from the chair. "They're here!"

Carmen headed toward the door, a sudden thunder of feet in haste to welcome their guests.

Finnigan shook his head and followed quickly after. He was vaguely confused, Carmen had not acknowledged the momentary absence.

You were asleep, who knows how long Carmen was really gone...

Finnigan brushed the thought away and ran his fingers through his hair. It had been too long since he'd seen Flynn. He wondered how he looked. He braced himself for the rush and confusion. Hardened against the flip in his stomach that always accompanied the thoughts of socializing with his younger brother.

It sounded as if they had entered through the east wing. Caden's voice boomed from somewhere below and echoed off the tapestried walls.

That was the problem with this house. Anyone could be anywhere, the walls distorted the truth at every possible junction. Finnigan followed the sounds. He had trained his mind to ignore the illusions and to adjust for the discrepancies.

He'd lost Carmen again, this time in the physical realm. There were many secret doors and hidden corridors, revolving bookcases and false floors, it was easy to slip off through a shortcut without a sound.

Finnigan adjusted his rings as he strolled, straightened his cuffs, his collar. Another anxious hand ran through his hair of its own accord.

What am I doing?

When Shadows Creep

He would only delay the inevitable with his spastic grooming.

He voyaged down the wide, sweeping marble staircase. Each tread was warm and worn and glowed in the light of the chandelier that demarked the exact center of the manor. His eyes traced the path of wet footprints that crossed the large entry. They came straight from the east corridor as he had guessed, and into the south.

"Of course, you horrid, messy beast," he cursed Caden. It would somehow become Finnigan's responsibility to clean up the mess that Caden had left behind, as it always did. The Caldwells were far less particular than the Freemonts when it came to their environment. One of these days, Finnigan was going to be driven to just throw Caden and his assorted messes off the nearest cliff and be done with it all.

Voices came from ahead. The bright glow of the fire in Carmen's office spilled into the hall. He swept past the framed portraits of long dead Caldwells; they all had the same angular faces, and the dark, deep hazel eyes. Eyes that stared at him as he hurried by.

The thought crossed his mind that he must be delaying the inevitable in his slow walk through the manor. It was better to get this over with, and finally say hello to Flynn. He stumbled at the threshold, paused, waited for some sign that he should enter. "You look exhausted, Flynn, was the trip so terrible?" Carmen's voice sounded pleasant enough.

There was no note belying any concern, as it had only hours before.

Finnigan put a hand to the door, attempted to envision Flynn inside. The response was much raspier that he expected, the voice lower than remembered.

He sounded old to Finnigan, as if more than five years had passed. Perhaps ten, twenty. But he knew, he knew deep down, it was that house that had done it. It had to be.

"Your brother's driving must have taken several years from my life if that's how I look."

Carmen laughed in response. Finnigan could almost see the glad-handing, the shoulder-clapping.

Ah, how funny it must be.

Finnigan rolled his eyes.

"How long are you going to lurk, then, Finnigan? I know you're outside the door. As usual." Caden's voice accosted him from within the room. A round of laughter punctuated the accusation.

Finnigan almost turned tail and fled down the hall. His skin had grown cold despite the warmth of the Manor. There was something else here, too. Once he had stopped focusing on the others and his muscles relaxed, he could feel it. A lurking in his gut that had nothing to do with his lunch.

The door swung open, and Carmen stared at him intently. "What *are* you waiting for?"

When Shadows Creep

. . .

The Dark

It didn't like this place.

The warmth, the noise. Too much talking.

It hissed as it crawled, undulated. It packed itself tightly into the corner. It glared suspiciously at a spider that pattered off at the interruption, a half-eaten insect abandoned.

It longed for the whistling windows of the Freemont house, the frosted glass protecting them from the storms. But it had to follow him. It had to know, it had to remind him that he belonged at Freemont.

Not here. Not here.

Never here.

It had gotten as far as the golden rosy chandelier, the twinkling lights too bright, too sickly sweet for the eyes. It had grumbled, reversed directions.

Slipped through a grate in the wall, felt the way along under the floorboards. It crawled through a layer of dust and decay, reveled in the cool brush of it. It emerged through another iron-clad opening, having circumvented the brilliance of the central room.

Flynn's heartbeat pulsed up ahead, a hollow thud that guided the Dark to where it needed to be.

It needed to watch.

It would wait.

Flynn would sleep once more.

...

Finnigan

Caden should have warned them, should have called. This was a situation for delicacy, and Caden had not observed the basic guidelines of society. If he had, Finnigan could have arranged his face into anything other than poorly contained horror.

But he hadn't.

And now here he stood, gulping like a fish. He flushed and tried to change his reaction. "Flynn! You made it!"

A moment too late.

He stumbled over his words and feet, moved forward in an awkward attempt at a handshake, a hug, and their elbows knocked into each other. They almost smashed their foreheads together.

Flynn brushed a hand through the long side of his hair, a shock of white that ran across the left side, neatly divided at his part. It was so pale in the flicker of firelight that it seemed to glow, and was in stark contrast to the cherry red of the rest of his short, trimmed hair. It was a popular cut, but certainly not in those shades.

And his eye. *Oh*, his eye.

Faded to a blue-grey, a blinded shade. The pupil was glazed and frozen.

When Shadows Creep

It appeared as if one side of Flynn, the left side, had been permanently and irreversibly affected by some sort of horrible catastrophe.

Finnigan clicked his mouth shut, realizing he had been staring at Flynn for far too long.

Flynn smiled, seemingly unaware of his strange appearance. He turned to Carmen and Caden and thumbed toward the door. "I am exhausted, though, to be completely honest. Is there any chance my old room is still available?"

Carmen nodded warmly, ever the gentile host, and gestured toward the door. "Please, let's walk. I'll show you where the linens have moved to since you left. I'm so sorry I didn't prep the room in advance, I was worried Caden wouldn't be convincing enough."

A smile flashed in Caden's direction, a laugh in response from Flynn, and then they were gone, the door pressed firmly closed behind them.

Finnigan wheeled toward Caden, "What the HELL happened to him?!"

Chapter Five

Flynn

Another day, another cage.

Flynn thudded his head against the pillow, cursed his belief in Caden.

I should have just dug in and stayed. Made them send the whole family after me.

He rolled over.

Rolled back.

Flipped the pillow.

Sighed.

Laced his fingers across his chest.

Kicked off the blankets.

Shivered.

Pulled the blankets back up, curled into a ball, pulled the covers over his head.

There was a knock at the door.

"Go away."

When Shadows Creep

"Come on Flynn, don't be mad."

"I said *go away!*"

Caden cracked open the door, peered around the jam. "That wasn't so bad, was it? No one freaked out, and you got a nice warm bed out of it. Your own room? What's the problem?"

Flynn sat up abruptly, brushed the hair from his face, and glowered at Caden. He crossed his arms, leaned against the headboard and refused to answer.

Caden threw his head back and loudly sighed. He pushed the door all the way open and shuffled into the room. His hands were jammed into the pockets of a thick, ruby red housecoat. Matching slippers completed the ensemble.

Flynn raised an eyebrow.

"It's seven in the morning on a Sunday, excuse me if I didn't get dressed up for you," Caden smirked.

Flynn didn't rise to the bait and remained angrily silent, his body humming with barely disguised wrath.

Caden sat on the edge of the bed, and the mattress sunk beneath his bulk. He picked invisible lint from the immaculate bedspread. He clasped his hands and waited.

Caden looked at his hands in shock. "Look at that! Still, not on fire." He waggled his hands in Flynn's direction.

Flynn huffed, "One of these days, Caden. I promise. Just once. It'll happen. Then what?"

"I'll take you out for a celebratory dinner."

That broke the anger for a moment, and Flynn grinned from ear to ear. He pulled his knees up to his chest and wrapped his arms protectively around them. "Did you see the way he looked at me?"

"You know, Flynn, I've spent all night thinking the exact same thing. Carmen isn't one to fudge the details, and I know that *I* walked into Freemont House knowing *exactly* what I was walking into."

Flynn frowned down at his feet and clutched his knees a little tighter.

Caden smiled encouragingly, "You know, it's been a long time. I'm not even certain Finnigan knew you were coming. You know how he leans toward the dramatic. That would have been his reaction no matter what."

Flynn brushed his hair from his eyes once more. "You and I both know that's not what shocked him."

Caden fell back across the bed in a *humph* of air and crossed his arms, rubbed his elbows. Flynn waited expectantly. "What do you want me to say? Why do you think Carmen sent me to get you in the first place? That is precisely why." Caden waved a hand in a circle at Flynn.

"You just gestured at all of me."

"Precisely."

"I had it handled."

"Sure, but, you got to be curious, Flynn. We don't age. We don't get sick, we don't die. And yet," Caden waved at the whole of Flynn once more.

36

When Shadows Creep

Flynn put his head against the headboard, staring up at the elegantly plastered ceiling. He had only lit the small bed-side lamp from a much closer century for his reading and the glow did not quite reach the corners. It created strange shadows in along the walls and where the light did not reach behind the wardrobe.

Flynn had an idea what lurked in the small space between the floor and curved legs of that heavy oak ward-robe. But he had yet to see it himself. Oh, how he longed to prove he was right.

"Listen, Flynn, a lot has happened in a very short amount of time. And we worry. Roman is off somewhere, we just want to keep an eye on you, okay? No big deal. And Finnigan has seen you now, so now he'll be prepared, right?"

"Where'd Roman go?"

Caden shrugged, failing to hide his concern.

"How does no one know where Roman went? It's *Roman.*"

"Yeah, well," Caden sat up and lumbered to his feet. He stretched, seemed to fill the room with his trunk-like arms. The stretch collapsed and he condensed in on himself, hands back in his pockets. "Come on, Finnigan has made quite the spread. It's probably an apology. Let's take advantage while it's hot."

Flynn stared at him for a moment before he scrambled from the heavy blankets. "Finnigan cooks?"

"Recently." Caden moved to one side of the hall to allow Flynn to keep pace with him. A casual stroll for one, an almost scurry for the other.

Door after door, room after room, portraits, paintings, pedestals of busts, suits of armor, on and on for what felt to Flynn like an hour.

Down stairs.

Up other stairs.

Through several locked doors.

Soon, the smell of bacon wafted through the air, the scent of coffee thick and cloying.

"Did my room need to be on another planet?" Flynn worriedly ran a hand through his hair.

Caden chuckled. "Carmen thought you'd like your peace and silence. You're used to it, at that house, right?"

"So you weren't quarantining me?"

Caden flattened his back against the next door. Flynn judged by the sounds coming from the other side that they had finally reached their destination.

"Us? You? Never!" Caden grinned and held it open, allowing Flynn to enter first.

The word *spread* did not quite cover the sheer volume of food that covered every flat, and several of the uneven, surfaces in the large kitchen.

Stacks of pancakes large enough for Flynn to hide behind. Great buckets of bacon, several carafes of coffee.

When Shadows Creep

Mountains of eggs cooked seven different ways. Sausages, waffles, home fries, a veritable fortress of buttered toast.

"How long did you say he'd been awake?" Flynn asked, eyes wide.

Caden snagged a sausage from a nearby tray. "Didn't. He didn't go to bed last night."

"Who's going to eat all this?"

Caden now chewed on a three-piece stack of toast, the bread engulfed in his large hand. He swallowed hard. "You, I guess?"

Finnigan popped up from where he had leaned into the stove, a large roasting pan in his hands. It was filled with ever more bacon. "Morning!" He called cheerfully, as he brandished an elegant plate of fine china he gathered from the stack at his elbow. "What can I load you up with?"

"Erm."

"Two of everything eh? Got to eat, Flynn, you're much too skinny."

As Finnigan busied himself at his task, Flynn took a hard step back and pulled Caden toward him. He beckoned him to lean down to hear his hiss. "What did you do with my brother? Who the hell is this?"

Caden smiled around the large slice of bacon he chewed. "Just enjoy it. Enjoy the food. Haven't eaten like this in ages!"

Finnigan hustled around the island with a large plate laden with food. He pushed serving platters out of the way to make room on the table. He pulled the chair out and gestured for Flynn to sit.

Finnigan waited for a full microsecond before he offered coffee, tea, and juice in three flavors.

"Finnigan, truly, this wasn't necessary, I-"

Caden's hand pushed him into the chair then pushed him toward the table. Caden leaned down, whispered in his ear. "Enjoy. I'll be back in an hour."

"Cade!"

He'd already disappeared, and the door behind Flynn's shoulder swung shut.

Finnigan had returned with an assortment of beverages, which he placed in precarious positions throughout the dishes that covered the table. The table groaned threateningly.

Flynn picked up a fork, hesitant, and speared a sausage.

Finnigan sat down on a nearby chair and stared at him expectantly.

The shock was gone from his face, but it had been replaced by Flynn's least favorite look. Morbid curiosity.

Flynn was almost finished with his hefty plate of food. He had eaten more than he ever would have imagined he could. Finnigan barely let him put down his fork before he started in with the questions.

When Shadows Creep

"Did you sleep well? Was it too loud? Too quiet?"

Flynn wiped his face with a nearby tea towel, carefully cleaned his fingers. "It was fine. I missed the sound of the sea, but other than that, yes, it was very, very quiet."

"Oh, the sea?" Finnigan rocked forward, placed his chin in his hands, expectant of more description.

Flynn did not oblige.

"I didn't realize Freemont House was anywhere near the sea. Must be lovely."

Finnigan cocked his head to the side, and Flynn could practically see the question sitting unasked on his tongue.

Flynn cleared his throat. "You would know if you'd ever come to visit."

Finnigan's face changed then, as his cheeriness turned sour. Eyes stormy, he sat back, arms crossed. Flynn recognized the move from his own repertoire.

"I'll clean this, shall I?" Flynn rose from his seat, the used cutlery and plate in his hand. His eyes passed over the remaining food, enough for a banquet, and shrugged.

"Flynn," Finnigan sighed.

Flynn shook his head and advanced toward the sink. A pile of dirty cookware loomed, a grease monstrosity for any seasoned dishwasher.

"Come on Flynn, let's just talk about this."

The back of Flynn's neck flushed red, he could feel the heat, the prickle under his hairline. He put down the plate as

41

gentle as he could, resisted the urge to smash it against the cast-iron mountain.

He turned, leaning against the sink. "There's nothing to talk about. I have *nothing* to talk to you about. I left. It was my choice. Mine. If you chose to interpret that in whatever bizarre twisted way you did, that was your choice. Now, please. I must go find Carmen and find out when I can leave this place."

Finnigan's face had turned beet red. He chewed his tongue.

Flynn headed toward the door Caden had left from, and was stunned to find it locked. He looked for the lock, grappled with the knob, and pushed a hard shoulder against it. The door didn't budge.

Flynn swung around to face Finnigan.

Finnigan merely grinned, "Caden did say I had an hour."

...

Carmen

"You did WHAT?"

"Locked them in together. You and I both know it's the only way to get them to play nice."

Carmen sighed and rested head in hand.

Caden looked uncomfortable for a moment, then

shrugged. He resumed the book he had been reading, his spot firmly marked by his thumb.

The sun had finally risen, golden and low, as it seemed to in the autumn, and had ignited the fallen leaves around the estate. The air was chilled, and steam rose from Carmen's coffee where it rested on the railing of the rambling back deck.

Carmen watched a deer pick its way through the edge of the forest. Its delicate legs lifted high over small bushes and around boulders as it roamed.

Caden's eyes rose from the pages. They followed Carmen's sightline, and together they watched the animal meandering through the overgrowth.

"You know the property is getting overgrown when this happens," Carmen sighed.

Caden had returned to his book, but closed it, now, and placed it face down on his lap. "There's so few of us now, Carm, there's nothing that we can do. It's all too much. It's not like the humans realize how far this property goes. It might as well be a magic wardrobe... it can afford to be overgrown, at least for now."

Carmen's lips pursed in response. "It's too easy for things to slip in without our notice when the grounds look like this. Trespassers. Hunters. Other things that go bump in the night." Carmen raised an eyebrow in Caden's direction.

He threw his book onto the stone topped table that sat between their chairs and twisted toward Carmen. "Do you think that It followed us?"

"It had too much to lose, letting Flynn go the way that It did. It was too easy."

Caden frowned, and his fingers groped at the lump on the back of his head where it had connected with the floor. "I don't even quite understand what *It* is. It looked like it was just made of shadows, just a darkness with a density. How could it even keep him there?"

Carmen gestured that he dip his head, and made a brief inspection of the injury, and Caden winced at the touch.

"It kept you from getting too smart-assed, didn't it?"

Caden pushed Carmen's hand away and glared,

"This "Darkness" flew at me abruptly, and my obviously less-than-optimal balance had overcompensated."

"Well, don't be too afraid of The Dark," Carmen grinned wide and toothy. "Let's be honest, we were both expecting a little more bloodshed. You did get off easy, I think."

Caden grumbled and turned back to the woods. "Do you think we'll know? If it crosses the borders? If it gets in the house?"

Carmen leaned forward and grabbed the coffee from the railing, took a hearty sip and considered a response. "To be perfectly honest Caden, I believe it's already here."

When Shadows Creep

...

Flynn

Finnigan knelt on Flynn's chest and dumped a platter of scrambled eggs square onto his face. Flynn sputtered and kicked the table hard enough to dislodge a large and heavy silver bowl of home fries onto Finnigan's back, who reeled away at the blow.

Flynn wiped the eggs from his face and sat up. He kicked out with his heels as he scrambled for purchase and pushed himself through the mess of breakfast foods strewn across the floor.

Both men sat silent, faces red, in their respective corners. Finnigan wiped the sweat from his brow and a smear of sticky syrup from his cheek. Flynn pulled a pancake from under where he sat, looked at it in disgust, and chucked it aside.

Finnigan laughed. It was a quiet rumble that grew, louder and louder until he wiped the tears from his eyes. The burst of laughter continued to spill forth in great waves until he fell over.

Flynn looked at him, incredulous.

"Oh God, Flynn. Seriously. How old are we?" Finnigan gestured around the room, the walls and ceiling coated in flung food and cold coffee.

45

Flynn trembled, then broke, and his laugh joined Finnigan's. Flynn put his face in his hands. "Finnigan, what did we do? This will never work."

"Oh it's fine, we'll clean it up, we always do." Finnigan hoisted himself up and extended his hand toward Flynn.

Flynn accepted it, stood up, and hugged his brother. There was more meaning in this simple gesture than there had been in the mammoth breakfast that Finnigan had prepared. It was too bad that he had already decided to leave. There was nothing more to be built between then, but at least he could rest easy now with the thought that they'd be parting on far better terms. "No, Finnigan. I mean us. Being back under the same roof again. It never worked before, why would we expect it now? I will be leaving. There's no way I can stay here. I shouldn't have even come back here."

Finnigan's expression sobered and he turned away, hands resting on the tabletop in a pool of spilled cream. "I get it, Flynn, I do. I know we didn't part on the best terms. And we didn't exactly reconnect last night, or this morning, any better. But I promise I'm different now. Right? Can we just… forget this? Start fresh?"

Flynn stared at Finnigan, and his good eye took in the details of how he'd changed over the years. There was a new bit of gray at his temples, and the dark beard he had grown.

Flynn's other eye, however, saw far more than that.

This eye could see the dark. In people, in things, in places. And it watched the ripples of shadows that curled around Finnigan's muscled forearms and coursed around his neck. It saw the cage around his heart that thrummed, dark and cold. No matter what Finnigan said, or did, that eye could see. There, around his heart, where his deeds had changed him over many years.

Flynn knew he would never truly change back to the man he once was. He choked back the words he wanted to say, and allowed his lips to curl into a smile he didn't feel,

"I will give it a try, if you will. A fresh start, as you say. But after we clean up. I believe Carmen will kill us if this kitchen stays this way."

Finnigan nodded, and they began to clean, attempting to find a good place to start and soon they began to find their rhythm. Flynn kept a careful eye over his shoulder, though, any time he had to turn his back.

It wouldn't do, to forget the dark.

. . .

The Dark

It had found its way to a window, had nestled behind the curtain and clung to the rod. It watched the two that had retreated outside.

Fresh air, a horrible thing. It *cleansed.*

Especially out here, where the trees were still alive inside and the sea was far, far away.

It shuddered.

It missed the sea. The depth and the dark. It could feel all else below. Down, down, where it would never be found. The Dark made sure of it. Made sure the humans were crushed, that their air was gone, the pressure far too much for any of humanity's advancements It gave the Dark a thrill, when they questioned why, and how, they couldn't proceed any farther. Their math was correct for all but one variable.

The Dark.

And the deep would be kept.

Because it was *ours*. That cold. That dark. Farther than the moon for the humans and forever out of reach, as long as The Dark had anything to say about it.

A twist of excitement shivered through its form.

A cloud scuttled past the sun, a temporary dim, and a bright, and now gone.

It winced.

Flynn had been locked where it could not reach, could not follow. The heat of that room was too much, so it had decided to follow the other one. The big one. The one that had stolen Flynn away from the Dark and the truth and the whispered promises in the night.

It had tried to connect with Flynn and his soul in the small hours of the morning when the great heart of the manor had settled and only ghosts wandered the halls. But

When Shadows Creep

Flynn was different here. *Stronger.* Something about being in the Manor changed him from the Flynn who It knew back at the Freemont House.

His mind had shut It out.

This would not do.

The Dark scuttled away from the window.

The other one had turned this way as if it had sensed what stared out from behind the thick glazed glass.

It hissed and twisted as smoke along the wall, along the ceiling.

There was too much anger there. Flynn must be done now with his brother.

Delicious.

But it was all It needed to find a crack in Flynn's façade. Flynn would let the Dark in again.

And he would dream.

Chapter Six

Flynn

Carmen shone a small light into first one of Flynn's eyes, then the other, and jotted a short note on the pad next to Flynn's hand. Reflexes had been tested, blood had been taken and bottled up in tiny labeled vials, then packed into a padded envelope. Carmen had already been through several pages of notes and hadn't uttered a word outside of instructions.

Flynn scratched at his bare collarbone. His skin pimpled into goosebumps and the hair on his arms stood angrily, frigid in the subterranean room as he sat shirtless, and waited for a suitable time to speak.

Something about Carmen made you feel as if you needed permission to break the silence.

But of course, Carmen was old, far older than any of them, and maybe it was merely respect that made them all hold their tongues.

When Shadows Creep

Carmen stepped back, chin in hand, and pondered the next move. "Do you think there's anything I've missed?"

Flynn shook his head, shrugged his shoulders, and reached for his shirt.

"Wait!"

Flynn paused, one arm successfully through his shirt, head encased in fabric, and his elbow caught up in the other sleeve. "What?" He said with a mouthful of shirt.

Carmen stepped forward and pulled the shirt from his head. This trapped his arms, extending them in front of his body to the point where his elbows touched.

"Lean forward," Carmen ordered.

Flynn felt delicate fingertips on the knobs of his spine and twisted his head to look at what held Carmen's interest.

"Strange," Carmen muttered and straightened Flynn's shoulders from where he tried to turn and look. "There are dark spots, they were faint when you sat straight, but as soon as you bend, they darken. Like bruises. But on every single one of your vertebrae."Flynn shuffled uncomfortably. This was something new. The change in his appearance, his hair, his eye, it couldn't be avoided. He saw it every time he looked in the mirror. He knew the freak he had turned into. But this was something else.

His mind reeled with the thought, was it inside him? Were the shadows of the Freemont home living inside his body, twisted around his bones and crawling around in his skull, a nest of vipers waiting to be unleashed? He knew what his eye saw, he knew the twists of darkness he could see around others, but how could he miss it entwined with his own self?

Flynn's skin crawled, and he resisted the urge to scratch at his arms, his back, and his stomach. He wanted to dig down and pull it by the tail and ask it why, why him, why now? But a small little thought niggled away at the base of his skull.

What if the shadows were just him? What if he caused them? This was all for nothing.

But if they were something… but a part of him…what if the shadows weren't evil at all?

Words pierced his silent reverie and he raised his head to listen. "I've never seen anything like this before." Carmen's fingers ran down his spine once more, and he was unable to keep from shivering.

Carmen seemed to snap from the reverie, and pulled the shirt back over his head. Back in the warm flannel he'd dressed in when roused from his bed by Caden, Flynn rubbed his arms and sat back. The chill of the room felt deep in his bones.

"It'll be at least four days for the bloodwork to come back. Hopefully, we'll have a better idea of what's going on then, hm?" Carmen jotted a few more notes down and stepped back.

When Shadows Creep

Flynn stared until Carmen looked up at him once more.

"You can handle a week with us, right? I know you and Finnigan are off to a rough start. But I promised you if we found nothing, if nothing changed while you were here, you could leave."

Flynn shrugged and looked away, stared off at a much farther distance than the floor.

"You know I'm good for it, not a single Absolute on either of my hands. My word has always been enough through the years, for everyone." Carmen's hands were held out as proof.

Flynn glanced at them briefly but he already knew. Carmen had been, and always would be, the only constant in Flynn's life.

He excused himself from the room and closed the door quietly behind him.

. . .

Finnigan

Finnigan had found a place next to another fire, in another room, in another wing. He'd never seen this room or passed through its door.

He loved finding new rooms.

Caldwell Manor was never the same, day to day. It shifted through time, same as the property. Altered. Grew. Shrank.

53

Finnigan remembered a time, around 1932, when the Manor had decided it existed only as a small carriage house. It had been difficult then, with nine of the family members at the time. There had been only three bedrooms with a large kitchen and a small parlor.

No formal dining at all then, no sir.

The thought brought a smile to his face. It had, thankfully, only lasted six months.

Maybe the Manor had been going through a bad time, or had just needed some time to think. Either way, it had rapidly sprouted up and out into a closer version of its current manifestation. Wings had grown along the compass directions. A sweeping, massive central staircase became the centerpiece of the Manor. An overwhelming chandelier and stunning mosaic mirrored ceiling were the most extravagant change he'd ever seen the Manor commit to.

Finnigan's eyes roamed the walls examining the details the house had added to this version of reality. The white wallpaper was dotted with dainty blue sprigs, and below the chair rail it met a smooth creamy wainscoting. Translucent blue curtains hung from dark wood rods and let the morning autumn light filter through. All the furniture was a mix of dark wood in a rich reddish shade, and a sort of periwinkle velvet. The Manor, as a rule, tended towards moody reds and heavy leather.

It was not a room he'd have ever chosen to spend his time in. But the unexplored nature of it appealed to him, and he wondered what it had been created for. The child's rocking horse in the corner unnerved him, the paint had worn away on the seat and the face as if by years of use and love. No children had ever been in the Manor, not so long as the Caldwells had been the Guardians.

And that had been a *very* long time.

One great glass eye—a vibrant blue shining against black paint— on the face of the wooden horse stared back at him.

The grandfather clock that stood in the corner of the room rang out a hearty, healthy sound and counted out the hours of the morning. It was only ten in the morning, but Finnigan had been awake for hours.

The meeting with Flynn had not gone as he'd expected.

Why did he assume that Flynn would forgive him so easily?

Several years ago...

Finnigan was roused from sleep by a trunk slamming shut. Confused, he twisted in the sheets. His pillow was jammed awkwardly under his arm and looked at the clock with bleary eyes.

"It's damned five-thirty in the morning. What's happening?"

The quiet room echoed back in response. He squeezed his eyes shut against the bright sun that had found its way between the curtains. He threw an arm over his face.

He'd had too much to drink the night before. He'd had too much twice over, if he was being honest with himself. He smacked his lips, groped for the water glass he usually left on the nightstand. He hit it with outstretched fingers and tipped it over the edge.

The glass shattered on the hardwood, splattered water in every direction. Finnigan groaned and moved to get out of bed.

His head was spinning. Pinpricks flashed behind his eyes and he lay back down.

A car door slammed.

Raised voices floated in from outside. Finnigan rolled toward the window, better to hear the argument beyond.

Sounded like Carmen. And Flynn?

It couldn't be.

Flynn hadn't yelled in the entirety of their lives. He was the most docile of the residents here, timid. Finnigan couldn't even remember the last time he'd seen Flynn angry.

And now, he was outside shouting, and apparently he had prepared to leave.

Leave? He can't leave.

Finnigan summoned the necessary strength to extract himself from the linens and took care where he put his feet on the floor. It wouldn't do to cut himself, not if he was needed outside.

Where in the Hell is Caden?

When Shadows Creep

Finnigan threw his housecoat over his pajama pants and headed toward the door. He grasped the handle and waited for the Manor to recognize his touch. He thought about outside, the bright sunshine, and the newly green shoots on the branches of the trees. He cleared his mind of everything except the warm smell of fresh spring earth and the buzz of honeybees. He opened the door.

As expected, the Manor had shifted slightly, transferred his door to an outer wall. He preferred a shortcut to the outside, and the action, rather than attempt to navigate the inner workings of the current Manor layout. It had only changed yesterday, and he had spent most of it drunk. He couldn't be expected *not* to ask the Manor to cooperate. What sort of Guardian would he be?

Finnigan winced as he stepped outside. Between the bright light and the sudden volume of the argument that rang in his ears, it was sensory overload to his poor, liquor-addled brain. He ran his fingers through his hair and attempted to assess the situation.

As he had guessed from inside, Flynn had packed his few belongings into a small blue rental car. It was an unfamiliar make to Finnigan, parked in front of the stone staircase that flourished its way across the front of the house. Finnigan marveled for a moment at the sweep of ivy and roses that covered the bright red brick. He hadn't been outside since the shift so he hadn't seen the Manor for what it now was.

Carmen leaned against a massive man-sized stone urn that was filled to burst with enormous fern-like plants that flanked the steps.

Flynn was red-faced but had quieted, as if he was waiting for a response. The silence hung in the air.

Finnigan chose this moment to stroll up, hands in pockets, and attempt to diffuse the situation.

"What's this all about, Flynn? Going on a trip?"

Flynn jolted and turned, looking surprised that Finnigan had made an appearance. "I'm leaving. I want to explore. I want to know more about this side of the world, see it all, and I'd be gone by now if Carmen hadn't stopped me."

A glare was thrown in Carmen's direction, who in turn shrugged it off.

"It's not safe for us out there. You can't be away from any of the Houses for too long, you'll tear away. You know that. I've told you that for years."

Finnigan nodded along with Carmen's words. "It's true, you can't go. This place, it's your connection to the undercurrent," he said, agreeing with Carmen. "It's where you belong Flynn, don't throw it all away for a misguided sense of adventure."

"That's what I've been telling him," Carmen gestured pointedly at Flynn.

Flynn's lip quivered with anger, and he turned toward the car.

When Shadows Creep

"Flynn, I'm telling you. You can't go. The Manor is a lifeline, not a prison sentence. You have to stay on the grounds. Things happen when Guardians leave." Finnigan stomped his foot and gestured wildly at the road beyond the Manor grounds.

"I think you're all lying. You know, all the Guardians that have left? The ones that *never came back?* I think they're happy. Safe. Enjoying their lives *somewhere else.* Anywhere is better than here, trapped inside a constantly shifting and twisting collapse of rooms and bricks from here until eternity. I can't do it anymore, I'll take my chances out there." Flynn wrenched open the door to the car and made to put one foot onto the car mat.

Finnigan strode forward and flung him back, slammed him against the rear door. "You can't do this Flynn, I won't let you."

"I'll do what I want Finnigan! I'm leaving." Flynn shoved Finnigan back, who tripped and fell heavily onto his back.

Flynn moved forward as if to apologize. He reached to grip Finnigan's outstretched hand and haul him to his feet, but he slapped Flynn's hand away. He got to his feet and squared his shoulders. "Listen to me Flynn, if you go, if you leave here? You're dead. You will die. And I won't care, because I know you did it to yourself. The second you cross off this estate, I don't have a brother. *I don't have you.* I will not stand here and mourn the loss of a brother who did not listen to reason and the advice of his elders."

His words had the same effect as if he had slapped Flynn clear across the face. Flynn physically recoiled from his threat.

Flynn stood for a moment, one hand braced on the roof of the car, the other dangled loosely at his side. His free hand was clenched into a fist, and he shook his head. "Fine, Finnigan. Have it your way, as you always do. It was nice, once, to be your brother."

The final word was punctuated with Flynn climbing in and slamming the door. Flynn gripped the steering wheel in both hands and rested his forehead against the wheel for a moment.

Finnigan stood, frozen.

The keys were turned, the engine turned over, the car was put into drive. And Flynn left.

And Finnigan kept his promise. His brother was dead, and as far as he was concerned, he could spend forever that way.

. . .

Carmen

Carmen knocked on the bottom of the passenger side door panel and watched Caden's legs jump.

When Shadows Creep

He shimmied his way out from under the car where he'd been inspecting the undercarriage. He threw a rag covered in a thick, black substance at Carmen's feet. "Well there you go, proof it was here."

Carmen's nose wrinkled at the sight of the rag. "Are you sure it's not just mud? It was an incredibly wet and awful day yesterday. Does it have to be residue?"

Caden rolled his eyes in response. "Do you see? Do you see how dark it is? The light isn't even reflecting off the surface of it. There's nothing darker, not that I've ever seen. Even oil isn't as black as that."

"Where'd you find all that gunk?"

"Tucked up over the axle. Must have just shoved itself in there and went along for the ride. Surprised it didn't get lost, fallen off somewhere along the cliffs."

Carmen toed the rag. "We'd have been better off if it had."

Caden dusted off his coveralls and unzipped them to the waist. He reached for the mug sitting on the hood of the car and took a large swig. He sat where his coffee had been and looked long and hard at Carmen.

The air had taken on that sparkling fall quality, and everything glittered against the brilliant blue of the autumn sky. The sunshine matched the golden leaves scattered in every direction. It reminded Carmen that winter would soon be there. That the cold and the dark would hold this area tight in its grip for many, many months, and there was only so much they could do against the evil that had followed Flynn.

Caden broke the silence. "I need to know what Roman's game plan was. What he told you we'd have to do before he left. I don't think he's coming back Carm, he'd have contacted us by now."

A wistful smile graced Carmen's lips. *Yes…it'd be easier if I just told him…*

Caden set his cup down and approached, rested his hands on Carmen's shoulders. "You don't have to carry it all. I know you've elected yourself as the leader since Roman left us high and dry, but that doesn't mean we can't help you. You'll tear yourself apart. It's bad enough we're down to just one of the Houses. With so few of us left, we can all pick up a little bit of slack to keep everything going strong."

Carmen looked tired, reflected in dark under eye circles and tightened features.

It was a moment before the words would come out around the stifled yawn of exhaustion. "It wasn't so long ago that we were *everywhere*. That the undercurrent came forth and pooled in so many more places. Strange places that became stranger when abandoned. It was all we could do to keep humans out of them, when they didn't belong, when the energy escaped.

Schools left shuttered during the summer heat. The echo of children's footsteps stampeding along the floor, thundering through echoes of time. Truck stops that rippled in the passing headlights. A mirage until a human entered. Wary of the one lone waitress pouring coffee to the same false people every night. We build—," Carmen coughed, then went on. "We *built*…so much to cover up what was there, to disguise it. My favorite was the basement of churches after hours. Usually, on a weekday, long after the ladies knitting group had cleared off for the night, the undercurrent would seep through the cold stone walls of the furnace room. The lights would flicker in the vestibules, the sole soul left behind was a disguised Guardian, dressed as a groundskeeper.

"Summer camps in the winter, the cabins ringed in frost. Stadiums when the last fan has left for the season. Ruins of old farmhouses, which the ground had almost reclaimed. We've lost so, so much. The undercurrent dried up. Those places lost their glimmer and returned to what they once were. Or faded away entirely, their Guardians returned from where they came."

Caden squeezed Carmen's arm in reassurance. Carmen could feel another vision creeping in, stronger than ever, and the words hurt when they spilled out, laced with vinegar and dread.

When they finally came, they were small and whispered, "I don't know what to do, and I don't know how to stop it."

Caden shushed gently.

"Rest Carmen. We'll discuss this later."

One of Caden's hands threaded into Carmen's hair, the other a steadying grip on Carmen's arm, as eyes rolled back and knees buckled. Carmen felt a hot burst of air in a sigh that came deep from within Caden, heavy with unshed emotion. That last words Carmen heard before oblivion took over were,

"Carmen, you're going to kill yourself. And then where will we be?"

. . .

Flynn

Flynn could see Carmen and Caden speaking outside. Caden had presented a dirty rag to Carmen, and then Carmen had retreated into the undercurrent. He couldn't quite fathom this strange turn of events, what the significance was, and why Carmen had felt the need to slip away.

He'd only ever seen Roman do it, and that was rare in itself.

He wasn't even certain Finnigan *could* do it.

Caden was much too much of a beast for him to have even attempted doing it.

And Flynn?

Well, how else had he survived so long outside the Caldwell Manor?

When Shadows Creep

That's what the others didn't seem to know – or maybe understand. The Freemont House had called him for a reason. And that reason was that it was one of the Houses. He was shocked that Caden hadn't picked up on it when he was there. He'd picked up on the Dark well enough, why not that? Couldn't he feel it? The great, thrumming energy that filled every corner of The Freemont House?

Wonderful, wonderful. A heartbeat between the worlds.

Of course, the Freemont House was not a shifter. It had been stable since he'd been there, but he was sure that it was only a matter of time before it started to change. There was something about the energy, the way that time passed when a house became a *House*. It was more than a day, a week, a year, it was all the weeks and all the years that ever could happen and ever had happened existing simultaneously. It was the fabric folded between time and space that caused the Houses to adapt to the necessary patterns of the multiverse.

And as far as Flynn was aware, none of the Guardians had quite figured out the *why* behind it all.

But Flynn was the one who had found it, this House that no one else knew about. He nurtured it, cultivated it for what it was. The trickle that it had started off as had become a mighty pool.

Being away from Caldwell Manor certainly was not the reason his hair and eye had begun its decay. They couldn't, they wouldn't—and *he wouldn't let them*—blame Freemont

House for that. It was his, and his alone. If Carmen and Caden and Finnigan, and hell, even Roman, couldn't understand that?

Well, he certainly wasn't going to share.

Despite the large breakfast he'd had, Flynn's stomach began to rumble. He shushed it and decided he would explore the Caldwell Manor. If he was going to stay here for an entire week, he might as well know the nooks and crannies and shortcuts of its current representation. Why not? No sense staying here in this room.

As he wandered, he realized just how many portraits framed the walls this time. A short walk showed him no less than thirty different renditions of the Caldwell family. Straight-nosed and dark eyed, they ranged from lords and ladies adorned in regal finery and expensive jewels, to children, wide eyed and bushy-haired. Some were even elderly, many of the men in their military finest, medals pinned to their chest.

Flynn shook his head. *The Caldwells, what a fine bunch.*

He laughed, and the sound echoed down the long hall. To Flynn's eye, it appeared to have lengthened since he first stepped foot inside.

He looked again. No, it had definitely lengthened.

The hall was several times longer than when he first crossed the threshold. A quick turn behind him and he realized the room where he had been spying on Carmen and Caden in had disappeared entirely.

When Shadows Creep

Flynn frowned, and turned back, to see the hall had turned into a dead end. It was nothing more than a dusty corner, the carpet worn and ragged. No pictures decorated these walls; the dark paneling was completely bare. A cold, hard shiver ran down Flynn's spine. He gently rested a hand against the wall to ground himself to where he was within the Manor.

The wall felt as fire, and he quickly pulled his hand away. He stared at the place his hand had touched, the outline of his hand burned into the wood.

"What the hell?"

The hand print faded away, as quickly as water dried under heat. Flynn bit his lip and pressed two hands to the wall in an attempt to recreate the effect.

This time he jumped back, his hands steaming, the wall too hot to touch. He stepped away from the wall, afraid to touch it, and turned back from the direction he had come.

A door of whitewashed wood sprung up in front of him. He gingerly touched the knob.

It was icy to his touch. But he gripped and twisted and pulled it anyway in a sudden desperate need to get out of this ever-shrinking space.

Beyond the door was nothing but darkness. An ever-black, ever-dark. So ebony that the light from the dim sconces did not penetrate past the doorjamb.

The Manor had never done this to him before. And he had no idea what to do.

Chapter Seven

Caden

Carmen awoke suddenly and scrambled off the bench, starling Caden. He had slipped into a dreamless doze, lulled by the warmth of the pre-winter sun and crisp country air.

"What's the matter, Carm?" He rubbed at an eye, stretched an arm across the back of the bench.

Carmen's head cocked towards the Manor, eyes panicked. "It's found him, Caden."

"What?" Caden jumped to his feet and looked up at the windows, searched for any sight of Flynn beyond the glass.

The bright red shutters that framed every facing window slammed closed. The sound was like a gunshot crack that echoed across the fields of the estate.

"The Manor, Carm, what's happening?" Caden turned back to Carmen, eyes wide, but the driveway was empty. Carmen had already raced up to the wide double mahogany doors with their brass star-shaped knobs and had started to batter on the wood.

"Finnigan! Flynn! Someone! Open the door!"

Caden rushed the steps two at a time and threw his full weight against the door, though the knob refused to twist in his hand.

"Finnigan! Please! Can you hear us?!" Fists rained against the door in succession.

Carmen sank to the floor, face in hands, and back against the door.

"Carmen, can't you speak to the Manor? It will listen to you?" Caden stared down at Carmen and gestured at the doors. "Come on, get your hands on it, go on, just talk to it."

Carmen twisted around, hands placed flat against the wood. With forehead against the brass mail slot, Carmen focused on the warmth beneath. The heartbeat beyond the cold air outside. A whisper in the air.

Carmen turned, looked up at Caden, eyes full to the brim with unshed tears. "Did you hear that?"

Caden shook his head.

A crow burst from the trees, a shadow against the flame of the leaves, its caw thundering through the silence.

The doorknob turned a soft click and opened a tiny crack. It was enough.

Caden shouldered his way through. The Manor had sent him directly to the center chamber, where the staircase twisted and the chandelier glittered.

"Which way?"

Carmen was already at his side, and pulled at his elbow. "Up, it's up there Caden."

The pair thundered up the stairs, only to be met just beyond the landing by a solid wall. There hung a portrait of a Caldwell from the 1300's that blocked their way. There was a sensual smile on her lips and a glitter in her eyes, a joke untold.

Both Carmen and Caden stood, gape-mouthed in shock when Caden heard the voice from the other side of the wall. It was tinny and small, and a rapid hammering came through, a vibration of the painting.

"Flynn?" Caden whispered.

The ground rumbled beneath their feet.

"A shift?" Carmen yelled the question, it wasn't time for one, and for certain, not the place. Flynn could end up anywhere.

Caden shook his head, took a step back. "There's got to be a way around, or through."

Carmen hammered on the wall. "We're coming for you, Flynn! Don't worry! We'll get you!"

The hammering on the other side stopped.

"Where'd he go?"

"Flynn!"

When Shadows Creep

...

Finnigan

"Flynn?"

The door to the strange blue room had opened and revealed a disheveled and confused Flynn on the other side.

Finnigan dropped his feet where he'd had them propped up on the arm of the couch and put down his glasses. "What have you been doing?"

Flynn stood silent and still as a quiet vibration ran through him.

Finnigan approached Flynn, gripped him by the elbows. "Flynn? You're cold and shaking, here, come sit."

Finnigan led Flynn to the couch and forced him to sit down. He grabbed a throw blanket and wrapped it around Flynn's shoulders. He knelt down in front of Flynn, snapped his fingers in front of his face. "Earth to Flynn, come in Flynn."

Flynn's shaking hand passed through his hair and sorted out the long white strands onto their correct side. His eyes flicked up to connect with Finnigan's. "Where am I?"

The tension left Finnigan's shoulders and he settled back on his haunches. "What, the Manor giving you a scare? You should have remembered how quickly it likes to change, especially when someone new is around. I've just found this room, spent some time in here, nice, isn't it?"

Flynn's eyes stopped their rapid-fire search of the room and settled on the rocking horse. "What's that doing here? In fact, what is this room doing here?"

Finnigan settled down more from his crouch to sit on the sofa and rested a hand on Flynn's knee. "Flynn? Are you okay? What are you talking about?"

Flynn threw off the throw as if it had begun to crawl against his skin, and scrambled to his feet. "This room doesn't belong here. It's…this room, it's…"

Finnigan approached Flynn with caution, he meant to take him by the elbow to push him back down on the sofa. The blood had left his face and he looked as if he'd collapse at any moment.

"It's alright Flynn, just breathe. What about the room?"

Flynn sat heavily down on the arm of the couch, took another slow and careful look around the room, and nodded. Whether to himself or to Finnigan, Finnigan couldn't figure out. The grandfather rang out, startling Flynn. Finnigan waited.

Carmen and Caden burst through the door with enough force to bounce the knob off the wall, and it rang with the force like a tin bell.

Flynn turned to look at the strange interruption, a sudden fear in his eyes. Finnigan leaped up at the disturbance, put himself between Flynn and the door. When he realized it was only the Caldwells who had stormed in, he simmered. "What was that all about?"

When Shadows Creep

He wheeled toward Flynn, "Does it have anything to do with what you were about to tell me?"

Flynn nodded.

Carmen gestured encouragingly and waited for Flynn to speak. Caden stood by, his hands clenching and unclenching, still riled for a fight that never came. Caden stood in the doorway, where Finnigan and all the rest knew it was safest to stand when the Manor was considering a shift. It prevented being pushed into one room or the other, and ending up at the opposite end of the Manor than you'd started. The house would only change around you, behind where you looked. Finnigan had already noticed out of the corner of his eye that the wallpaper in the hall behind Caden had changed three times since they had stormed in. Finnigan did not want to bring attention to it.

The Manor was agitated.

Flynn finally spoke. "This room is from my house. The second floor, third door on the right in The Freemont House... somehow, now, it's here."

. . .

The Dark

It felt a giddiness it had not experienced in an unimagined length of time. Flynn had shown it things, showed him sneaks and peeks it had never dared know before now. The

Freemont House had just been a small place, a cold place, where things like the Dark could creep and linger, safe from prying eyes. But the cracks in the narrow spaces between realities had widened, a little more, all the time. Just a little more, and it had changed the Freemont House into what it had always been destined to be.

And exposed the Dark to the energy and power of the undercurrent.

And it was more than the Dark could have ever hoped for.

But Flynn was the key to that place, to where the Dark could slip in and out between the here and there. Following Flynn had been the best decision it ever made.

It had been afraid at first, when it realized it was blocked from Flynn's mind and his sleep and his dreams. But it could see now that it was only temporary. Because here, with the Caldwell Manor open and alive with the assistance of the Guardians, the Dark could tap in.

It could *change* things.

It could play with Flynn's head. With all of their minds, and have plenty left to grow.

And grow it would.

When Shadows Creep

...

Carmen

"What do you mean, this room is from the Freemont House?" Carmen asked.

Flynn gestured around the room. "This wallpaper? I added it. Over a particularly awful shade of pea soup, I must say. That clock? Found it at a rummage sale three miles down the road from the market I go to on Saturdays. That rocking horse I dug up from the cellar myself, cleaned it up. I replaced the eye!"

Carmen looked disturbed, and passed a concern glance to the others as Flynn continued.

"I restored every bit of it. Look! Look over here, I guarantee you, penciled on the side of the mantle will be the measurements I needed for the curtains. I didn't have any paper handy, look!" He strode confidently over and jabbed at the words with his finger. Flynn slumped against the wall, exhausted and bewildered.

"How does this happen, Carmen? How can it just be here? I left it hours away on the edge of the sea. What could it possibly be doing here?"

Carmen sank slowly onto the sofa, confused and tired until a sudden thought struck. "Flynn, you've been gone for so long... How? Did you find yourself access to the undercurrent? Somewhere out of the way, close by to the

Freemont House? An abandoned mill maybe? An old grave-yard? Somewhere you could visit, and not be disturbed? Is that how you've survived away for so long?"

Flynn laughed, an odd sound in the stressed atmosphere in the room. It carried past where Caden stood near the door. It wavered down the hall, a desperate echo. Flynn recovered with a click of the jaw and shook his head, looking down and away from the others.

Finnigan stood and pointed at Flynn. "You found yourself a soft spot at Freemont House. You weren't just renovating it, you were *prepping* it! You became its Guardian, didn't you? You helped it grow into a proper House. Is that what you did, Flynn? Traded one prison for another? Did you even know what you were doing out there?"

Carmen's mouth popped open in shocked horror.

Caden spoke before Carmen could think of what to say. "You can't just play with the undercurrent. It's far too powerful. Look at this place, look at the Manor, it locked us out from you. We were powerless to stop it. It wouldn't take much for it to pull you under and you'd drown. Trapped in the reality the rest of the Manor resides in. We couldn't do anything to save you if that had happened." Caden blanched at the end of his diatribe and looked for a moment as if he might vomit.

Carmen gestured for Flynn to sit down on the sofa, and he wobbled over, almost collapsing at Carmen's side.

76

When Shadows Creep

"Flynn, be honest. We all thought that this," Carmen touched his hair, his face, tilted his face toward the light. "We thought it was because you left us. Not because you created your own place, found your own access to the undercurrent."

Flynn shrugged and turned away from Carmen's grasp, and put his head in his hands.

Carmen rested a hand on his shoulder. The grandfather clock cheerily bonged its way through another hour. All four heads turned to look at it suspiciously.

Finnigan jolted straight out of his seat. "Please tell me that clock is broken, that it just makes that stupid noise whenever it wants, Flynn. Tell me it's broken."

Flynn hadn't broken eye contact with the clock, an eyebrow raised over his glazed and lightened eye. "No, I had a professional come in. Said it was in perfect working order. Never a wrong moment, that one."

"Then how exactly has…," Finnigan looked down at his watch and shuddered, "Four hours passed in what was only about a half hour?"

"Guys, I think you should come on out of there." Caden called over his shoulder. He was looking away from them, down along the hallway.

The wallpaper had shuffled again like a deck of cards, a hundred different colors, and textures. Light and bright, dark and dim, as if days and days had passed outside the Manor.

It was as if all of Flynn's energy had been consumed. He had lost the energy to stand. Carmen and Finnigan each took one of Flynn's elbows, and he sagged between them. They paused at the door.

"Um, so you think the way will shut if he leaves first? Or will it shut him in behind us?" Finnigan voiced the concern that had crossed all their minds.

Carmen palmed the door frame, ran a hand up and down the whitewashed wood suspiciously. "We'll fit if we all crush in tight together. Then we don't have to figure out the answers to those questions."

They each wrapped an arm tight around Flynn's body and pressed him against their sides. His arms slung across their shoulders, they pushed through together, Finnigan with his eyes squeezed tight.

The hallway ceased its violent spasms of transition the second they crossed the threshold. Caden offered to take Flynn, and not a moment too soon as Flynn's knees buckled beneath him.

"I'm going to put him to bed, this has been far too much for him I think," Caden said.

Carmen nodded, though seemed to be elsewhere, eyebrows furrowed, and gaze directly on Flynn. Carmen's head tilted in question,

"I wouldn't leave him, though. There should always be one of us with him. I'm not sure what the Manor is trying to do, but we won't ignore it. Caden, you'll take the first watch?"

Caden dipped his head once, and turned away, Flynn firmly flung over his shoulder.

Finnigan pinched at his nose, lowered his head into his hand, and inhaled deeply. "What has my little brother gotten himself into?"

They turned toward the doorway they had escaped to find the wall had rippled the door away. The air was now clear and calm, the charged feeling gone. The Manor had erased the wrongdoing to the Guardians and made sure they would not cross paths with that room again.

Carmen touched the wall gently where the door had been. The door was now replaced with a landscape painting, trees and fields and lush green, the roof of a house peeked over a hill, the sea beyond. "I haven't the slightest idea."

Chapter Eight

The Dark

It twisted away from the hallway, pleased by the effect it had on the Manor and its occupants.

It scurried through this vent and that, leaving a trail of smoke in its wake. It crawled along under floorboards and between the lathing. It wound around light fixtures and smeared its oily darkness in shadowy corners.

It followed the path that the large Guardian took, Flynn dangling unconscious from his shoulder. It hissed in excitement. Flynn was not asleep, his dreams would not come to his defense. The Dark would not be blocked.

Soon, the large one would stop and It could seek what it what it was looking for; nothing would stop it.

The large man stopped for a moment, struggling to adjust Flynn. He opened the door to Flynn's room.

Strange, the Dark thought. Flynn's room had not once shifted. The others slept in the rooms left behind each night. None of the others had a space to call their own.

When Shadows Creep

Flynn had his very own room at the house by the sea. He slept in the same place every night. The passage through to the undercurrent there, at the Freemont House, was young and wild. That house had not once shifted while Flynn lived there.

Whatever effect he had on the Freemont House also prevented this room from changing.

Flynn was an equal and opposite force to the forces at work within the Manor.

The trick must be inside Flynn's head. The Dark was sure of it.

It crawled through the crack between the door and the jamb, halting the light that passed from the bedside table to the hall. It was just a moment, but the large man carrying Flynn looked up.

Too slow. He would never catch the Dark.

It whispered across the ceiling and came to rest in the upturned glass of the chandelier. It looked down at where Flynn was laying on the bed. His hair was scattered in a halo of snow around his head, so light against his skin. He stared upward with his glazed eye, almost as if he watched the Dark.

Impossible. The Dark could see from his expression that Flynn knew no more that the Dark was there than where he was at this moment.

The Dark wondered if the illusion of the Freemont House within the Manor had finally broken Flynn. To see a place you knew existed far away, and in exact, stunning duplication to the very last nail, seemed to be even more than these world wanderers could handle. It recognized that this place, however changing, was only ever here, wherever here was. The Dark thought that for Flynn, the implications must have been far more devious than could ever be recognized. To the Dark, it appeared Flynn's mind had simply shut off.

Either way, it had enjoyed what its work had wrought.

It was pleasant to see what it could do when it was tapped into this new and wonderful power.

But this House was trying to push the Dark away. The Dark was an irritant, as sand to an oyster. And like that sand, it would grow into something beautiful.

Dark, but beautiful; a moonlit night upon this house; a curse upon this land.

It could grow; a fungus, a mold.

It would absorb and grow and change and find the next crack to the undercurrent. Then it would seep through all of reality.

But first, Flynn.

When Shadows Creep

Caden

Caden sank into the chair beside Flynn's bed. He had been certain that Flynn would be better off back at Caldwell Manor. He didn't think any of this would happen. Things had gotten so much worse.

Something was very wrong with Flynn. Caden could see it was well outside the realm of his understanding how far Flynn had fallen.

Caden settled his hands across his stomach, fingers laced together, and stared at Flynn. It had been surreal when he stood outside the door to that room. He had witnessed the fury of the Manor and the changes it had spun through, maniacal, and yet somehow methodical. It was as if the Manor was trying to shake something off, shake it out, upend the household and toss something away.

Caden wasn't certain it had succeeded, though. He was seeing things; a flutter at the corner of his eye. He still felt a strange sensation, like a tight grip on the base of his spine.

He swore he could feel fingers groping at his throat and his chest, spider-like up his legs.

It was a horrible, horrible, intense feeling that he could not shake no matter how hard he looked into the corners and under the furniture. No matter how many times he assured himself that nothing was there.

He swatted at his neck as if a mosquito and landed gently on his skin. His hand came back empty. He shivered.

If this is what it had been like for the humans, when they tried to stay at the Freemont House, he was not surprised that they had all turned tail. He had read up on the rumors when they discovered where Flynn had retreated. It was important to see what Flynn had got himself into, to be prepared.

Prepared for what, at the time, he'd had no idea.

Really, he still didn't.

It was like ghosts had taken hold of his mind.

"I'll have to speak with Carmen, to make sure these shifts are short. There's no way anyone can hold onto their sanity for long. Not with this constant malignancy lurking at the back of your mind," Caden muttered to himself.

His gaze snapped to the ceiling. He swore he heard a hiss, almost triumphant. But nothing lurked there.

Just another figment.

Caden could feel a headache beginning to buzz at the base of his skull. It wouldn't be long before it was a full-blown migraine.

Exactly what I need right now.

Flynn murmured in his sleep, then. He curled into himself, onto his side with his back toward Caden.

"He's so fragile," Carmen's voice came from the doorway. "He talks a big game, but he never really ever toughened up, huh?"

When Shadows Creep

Caden shook his head, eyes still glued to Flynn.

"You could end it, you know. Stop him being a problem."

He'd never heard Carmen speak that way about Flynn, not once. Not ever. Caden's head whipped toward the door. But the doorway was empty, the hallway dark beyond. A lamp far down the hall stuttered.

Caden turned back to the bed, adjusted the chair so he could keep the door in sight. He was suddenly very afraid to take his eyes off of Flynn.

. . .

Flynn

It was so foggy down in the garden. Flynn could barely make out where he walked. The cobblestone path he followed wound its way amongst the bushes and the dead garden beds lined with large river rocks. Despite the damp, freshly fallen leaves crunched underfoot.

Visibility was no more than a few feet in the inky gray garden. He held his hands out tentatively, worried that he'd trip or walk into something, anything. He wasn't certain exactly where he was, but he followed the path. He'd either end up at the burbling river that stretched along the western edge of the property— it was past the reach of the undercurrent and the whims of the ever-changing Manor— or he'd find the hardwood deck that stretched along the back of the house.

Flynn rubbed his hands against his chilled arms, feeling the moisture as it gathered in a slick sheen across his bare skin.

Why wasn't he wearing a coat?

He wrapped his arms about himself, trying to defend against the deep chill. His fingertips had turned blue.

A weak sun tried to push through the fog, no more than a subtle shift in the illumination around him.

A squawk erupted from the right side of the path. He looked over and spotted the crow as it took off from the large bush where it had been hiding.

Flynn stumbled, but caught himself on his knee and outstretched hand, and stood back up to assess where he could be.

The river was no more than a few minutes' walk from the back of the Manor, he should have easily reached it by now.

It felt as if hours had passed in this strange, heavy fog.

Flynn moved off the path, tried to find the edge of the forest, and nearly walked into a cherry tree. It was the same tree that graced the far back corner of the property every year with its bright pink blooms. This time of year, however, it was naked to the elements, flowers long gone, fruit long fallen from its branches.

When Shadows Creep

The crow now stood on a low branch, its eyes glittering like pebbles in the dark. As Flynn moved, the crow turned his head, watching him. He marveled at the sheer size of the bird. It was not a crow after all. His earlier assessment that it was a crow had been wrong. No, this... This was a raven. He'd never seen one in person, and certainly not this close. It hopped to a lower branch, his glittering eye now even with Flynn's. He took a hesitant step back.

The raven tilted its head in the opposite direction and made a short croak at Flynn's retreat.

Flynn froze, waiting to see what the massive bird would do. His hands were half raised, in case it decided to lunge and peck out his eyes or claw at his face.

It did none of these things, but extended its leg and released a round object it had been holding in its claw. The bird then launched itself into the air with a great beat of wings and a rush of air, and disappeared into the thick of the fog.

Flynn dropped to his knees in the cold and dripping grass. The wetness soaked through his pant legs as he fumbled amongst the yellow and brown leaves, looking for what the raven had dropped.

It's important, I need it. It's important, I need –

And there, nestled under a clump of clover, was the object.

He picked it up and held it out in front of him. It was cool in his palm, round and egg-like, but made of something far harder than eggshell. It felt like stone, smooth as polished marble. It was black. Far more black and dark and solid than anything he'd ever seen in the world. The light, meager as it were, did not reflect from its surface.

He wiped away the bits of leaves and grass trimmings that clung to its surface and pulled it close to his body.

This was special.

Flynn had no idea what it was, but he knew it was his now. A gift from the raven, and his responsibility to keep safe.

He dropped it into the breast pocket of his shirt and rested his hand gently on the lump that now lay over his heart.

Flynn stood and looked around. The fog had cleared and now all the stars shone down from the dark sky. Great, brilliant systems of stars streaked overhead, a thousand Milky Ways glittering from above. Flynn's breath coalesced into mist around his face.

It was so very cold.

The bushes and trees around him were lit with millions of fireflies, their eerie blinking green lights highlighting the path and the property surrounding him. But there was no mansion, no house, no building in sight. Nothing for forever in any direction besides trees and the path and the glinting light of the fireflies.

He inhaled a deep breath and pushed down the fear roiling in his gut.

It's okay. It's okay. You'll find a way home.

He spun, squinted in each direction and tried to determine if he could see anything, any clue or indication of which way he should go.

The thing in his pocket flared with heat when he turned around once more, so he stopped.

Maybe it knows where I need to go.

He tested his theory, and a turn toward the opposite path made a chill run through him. The sudden absence of warmth against his chest was like being dunked in cold water.

Flynn turned back towards the warmth, and began his walk. Toward what, he didn't know. But he trusted it.

Chapter Nine

Caden

Caden wiped at his eyes. The afternoon had slowly dripped into the evening, the dark coming earlier than ever thanks to the season. Flynn had begun to mutter in his sleep and had stirred Caden. He'd slipped into a doze a couple hours into his watch.

No more spirits had approached the door. Carmen had been in the room twice to check on him and had been confused by the apparition that Caden described.

Carmen had heard Roman speak of echoes, previous Guardians that had lived in previous versions and shifts of the Houses. They were mere shadows of their former selves, an imprint of an emotional time or outburst. With their energy trapped within the walls, they did not interact with current Guardians. And they certainly never offered input on what was happening in a House. They simply weren't on the same level of existence as the actual inhabitants.

When Shadows Creep

Carmen had not, however, seen or heard of an echo in the Caldwell Manor. And she had expressed concern that this was something far different.

Finnigan had also popped in at one point, to inform him he'd cover his shift at half past eight. The clock on the night table only read seven. Caden stifled a groan.

Flynn flipped over onto one side, suddenly, and cried out as if in pain. Caden slid from the chair and knelt by the bed. He had agreed with Carmen that he shouldn't "loom" or "lurk" over Flynn, as his size was prone to do. Neither believed that scaring Flynn right out of bed was the best treatment for whatever was wrong with him. So kneeling was his compromise.

Caden gripped Flynn's outstretched hand and made calming noises under his breath, as the cadence of Flynn's muttering slowed.

"I don't know where you went, Flynn, but it's alright to come back now, I think."

A fresh wave of unease passed over Caden, but he shook it off. A quick glance at the door assured him that they were still alone. A pattering sound, rain or rats, or something else made a dash overhead. Caden moved closer to Flynn.

Flynn's hand returned the squeeze of Caden's panic and he looked down to see Flynn looking up at him. "Jeez, Caden, why don't you just climb on in here with me? Give a man his space, huh?"

Caden dropped Flynn's hand as if he'd been stung and sat back on the floor, arms thrown over his knees.

Flynn groaned and push himself up to sit against the headboard and rubbed at his eyes. "What time is it? Why must you insist on waking so early every damn day?"

Flynn winced as he looked at the clock. "Seven? Really? Come on! How am I supposed to get any rest in this house?" Flynn flopped down and pulled the blanket tight around him.

"P.M, Flynn. That's seven P.M."

Flynn tightened the blanket for a moment, then flung it down in a puff of air. "You said what?"

Caden ran a hand through his hair and shook his head. "You've been unconscious for four hours. After we were trapped in that room and lost three. All in all, roughly seven hours unaccounted for in your day. Not counting wherever you went after breakfast. You could have also been trapped within a shift then, but we don't know that, and Carm doesn't think you would know either."

"But I was out there, in the garden, for the afternoon, and most of the night, it was the most beautiful night." Flynn's voice was small. Too small for conviction.

Caden shook his head. "No, Flynn, you've been here. I promise. You didn't go anywhere, I've been here in this chair this entire time."

When Shadows Creep

...

Flynn

Flynn reached into his pocket of his shirt and felt the stone in his pocket, warm against his chest.

A low rattle filled his ears. A warning sound.

Caden was staring at him, apparently unaware of the noise Flynn could hear, and completely ignorant of what Flynn kept hidden in his pocket. He withdrew his empty hand, wiped his eyes once more.

"I don't know, I must have dreamt it. It seemed so real. I thought I'd been walking out there forever. I followed that path but I couldn't find the Manor."

Caden continued. "It's okay. It was a strange day for all of us. You're awake now, though, so we should probably go find the others and let them know everything is okay. You can't be alone, though. Carmen doesn't think it wise for any of us to be alone as the Manor still hasn't settled down. Whatever ruffled its feathers about the room from Freemont House hasn't gone away. Can you feel it?"

Flynn looked at Caden strangely and shook his head, tight-lipped.

He wants the stone. He can feel it. He can't have it. I won't give it to him.

The thought crossed Flynn's mind with alarming clarity. It burned, deep down, and he hid the flame away.

Caden, unaware of what happened, pulled himself up to his feet and looked around. His eyes narrowed suspiciously at the light fixture above his head. "I swear, I kept hearing…I don't know, something. Up there somewhere?"

Flynn clambered out of bed and joined him. Together they stared at the ceiling. Flynn was the first to turn away, and he shrugged, pulling a sweater off the end of the bed over his head.

He headed for the door. "You've lived here for far too long, Caden. It was only a matter of time before you started imagining things."

Caden frowned as Flynn slipped around the corner into the dark hallway beyond. Caden hurried quickly after, as if panicked by Flynn disappearing from his sight.

. . .

Carmen

Carmen's forehead rested on the polished surface of the harvest table that took up two-thirds of the small kitchen. A sigh fogged the glossy wood.

Faded.

A door closed nearby. Carmen shot straight up and squinted at the newcomer. Confusion was replaced with joy as Carmen realized who it was. "Roman!"

The man dipped his shaggy gray head in response and

slung his heavy leather bag onto the end of the table. He pulled out a chair and sat with a loud thud. He crossed a leg and leaned back to inspect Carmen, a thick gray eyebrow raised over a bracing green eye.

Carmen sat forward over folded arms. "When did you return? How was it? How are the others?"

Roman raised a hand, shushing the flow of questions from Carmen. "There will be enough time later to discuss my time abroad, but first," Roman gestured around, "What is affecting the Manor so? Surely Flynn's return hasn't riled it up this badly? I've never seen it so excitable. It took me four tries just to get through this door, the knob kept switching sides."

Carmen looked at the door and watched it flip through several variations of varnishes and sizes and textures before returning to Roman's gaze. Carmen's hands shook, despite trying to keep them steady around the half-empty coffee mug that rested on the table. "Well, Flynn, he's back, as you know. As per your instructions," Carmen paused for a confirmation, a nod from Roman in return.

Carmen exhaled loudly and looked to the ceiling for support. There was a dark smear, a smudge or a scuff mark that marred the clean cream surface, and Carmen frowned at it before continuing. "And it seems that we should have been more worried than we thought. There was something there, at that house. Freemont House. Something dark. I think it may have been feeding off of him, or possibly the undercurrent. And it has followed him here."

Roman leaned forward, sleeves rolled up to his elbows. He was prepared, somehow, for whatever needed to be done. Carmen could see it on his face.

"What do you mean, it fed off the undercurrent? How did it have access?" He asked.

Carmen swallowed, hard. It suddenly became difficult to explain the oversight. They should have checked sooner. They should have known better. "It seems Flynn found a soft spot. The Freemont House is just that now, one of the Guardian Houses, no longer a regular building but now a place for the undercurrent to pool through. I thought the closest one was that truck stop, up on 53, the one that only appears between 2:17 and 3:45 am? But it appears he nurtured this one under our notice. And I think it's grown. And whatever it is that followed him here, it wants him for something. I haven't figured out what yet." Carmen ran a nervous hand across the edge of the table, afraid to see the disappointment in Roman's eyes.

Roman remained silent, processing the words that had shook more and more as they fell from Carmen's lips.

"It's much worse than I thought. I knew," Roman looked away, out the window, at the golden light pooling through the shockingly yellow leaves and into the kitchen. He continued, "I knew that something was wrong. I could feel him weakening, even from here I could tell that his life force wasn't what it once was. But I honestly thought he'd just been away for far too long. If I'd known that it was something else and that that something would follow him back here, I would have gone for him myself. Made sure that no one was in over their heads."

Carmen's head shook in disagreement,

"No, I should have known better, Roman, should have taken more precautions. Hell, I should have at least tried to visit him, made sure he was okay. But Finnigan was so insistent."

Roman rested a hand on Carmen's, and gave it a quick squeeze. "Finnigan is a domineering spirit. It would exhaust all of us to fight with him as much as he believes he needs to."

Carmen offered a quick smile in response.

It was true. Finnigan *was* exhausting. Quick to anger, quick to argue, even when he agreed. Hot headed, hot tempered, whatever you chose to call it, Finnigan defined it. But he was also loyal to a fault, quick to be injured by a poorly expressed comment, and defiant to the end. The best thing to do was to make decisions without him and deal with the fallout rather than delay by considering his opinion first.

If Finnigan was honest, as Carmen knew he would never be, he would have admitted that it was *hurt* rather than anger that fueled his estrangement from Flynn. Finnigan had felt rejected by his brother's insistence on leaving. He interpreted Flynn's departure as Flynn believing that death was better than spending one more moment in his brother's presence. Which hadn't been the case at all.

Flynn had felt captured and smothered throughout the many, many years spent in Caldwell Manor.

It wasn't their place to be here, the Freemont brothers, but the world of the Guardians was ever-shrinking. Roman had decided it would be better if the Caldwells and the Freemonts pooled their resources. The Manor was more than enough space and time for all of them to share.

Their original responsibility was a playground that only flickered into existence during every new moon, as long as it fell in October. October, the month when the winds blew strong and the leaves skittered across the broken tarmac. It would only appear that night, between nine and midnight, and it had been easy enough for the brothers to manage.

A small two-bedroom home skirted the web that the undercurrent weaved. It had been enough for years and years. On these dark moonlit nights the Freemonts would leave the house and spend those three hours on the swing set. Or perhaps perched on the top of the curving orange slide. That would be enough to deter any teenagers from crossing paths with the cracks in reality; to prevent any humans from falling through a shift.

When Shadows Creep

But one year, the playground didn't return. The glamor was gone, the empty lot remained empty, and something changed. The liminal space was no longer that, but dead. It no longer held the time or space or magic that abounded in the places between realities. They couldn't stay there anymore, not without access to the undercurrent. They needed that thinness of atmosphere and electricity to survive.

And so Roman came for them. And they followed, reluctantly, always hoping that maybe it was temporary.

But it was the wildness of the clouds billowing across the dark sky, of the icy air and the glitter of stars, and that thickness of shadows that had sustained Flynn throughout the days and years before they were no longer needed as Guardians.

And Flynn became broken by the absence of that wild.

So, he left them. He couldn't handle it anymore. He wasn't to be domesticated.

Maybe that made Flynn worse than Finnigan, as his differences lurked beneath a calm and gentle exterior instead of roiling across his surface, but none of that mattered anymore.

Carmen returned from reverie and met Roman's gaze. "There's a darkness about Flynn now. He sees us and the world differently than he did. It clings to him like smoke, an odor of brimstone. He's been touched by something, something that lingers. He has marks running down his spine, it's as if," Carmen choked and took a sip of cold coffee. Roman was patient.

"It's as if something is intertwined with him, at the very core of him, and I am so afraid." Carmen exhaled, long and loud and hard. It was a relief to put words to the feeling that had been curled up so deep inside. Carmen hadn't even voiced this opinion to Caden, worried about what he might think. Caden expected Carmen to remain strong, so that is all that would show. Outwardly, at least.

A scratching sound came from the ceiling as if over the plaster but under the floorboards overhead. Both Carmen and Roman looked up. A sudden chill made goosebumps run across Carmen's skin. The hair on the back of Carmen's neck stood up.

Roman was on his feet immediately, and headed for the door, Carmen in quick pursuit. For an old man— or at least, a man with the appearance of being old—he moved preternaturally quickly as he bounded down the hall. He knocked into a marble bust sitting precariously on a hall table, but managed to catch it at the last moment.

Carmen struggled to keep up. Roman climbed the central staircase two at a time, long legged. He slid to a stop at the plain unpainted door and waited for Carmen to arrive, panting behind him.

Carmen released the knife attached to forearm and wrist, using the spring-loaded button that launched it into open palm. It was a weapon all of them wore. Carmen nodded at Roman, who flung open the door.

Something slipped into the vent, the end of a dark so black it rivaled the starless night. Roman dove for it. His hands came up empty, but he scrambled at the screws that held the grate in place and pulled them from the floor in quick succession.

He made to reach an arm into the hole before Carmen grabbed his shoulder to stop him. "It could bite."

Roman looked incredulous for a moment and then sat back on his haunches. A patter of sound rang out under the floor and traveled to the next vent in the opposite wall. He sprang towards the vent, the penlight from his pocket now in his hand. He shone it directly inside.

The room was quiet except for the sound of their lagging breaths.

The air began to fill with whispers.

Quiet, they undulated, a fragment of words here and there, voices increasing in the air.

Roman spun the penlight around the empty room. But it was futile in his search for the source of the whispers.

"Are they echoes?" Carmen cried out, hands clamped over ears in an attempt to keep out the words.

Roman shook his head, panic in his eyes.

The room went silent.

They held their breath in response, in wait of what, Carmen didn't know.

A loud thud crashed down on the floor above, and their eyes met briefly, before they ran from the room and tried to figure out which way to turn. The central staircase only rose one floor, and they were at the top. The Manor needed to supply them with another route, another door.

There must be stairs, Carmen thought, to a third floor, hidden somewhere along this hall.

Roman closed the door they had exited, grabbed the knob, closed his eyes in quick concentration, and then flung it open.

Carmen had silently begged the Manor to give them a route, to help them find a way to the very thing that the Manor dreaded most.

It worked. The empty room had transformed into rising stairs, narrow and dusty with no lights from above to light their way.

Roman shined his flashlight up, highlighting the cobwebs and dust and dead things that lined the steps.

"I don't think we should go up there," Carmen puffed.

Roman shone the light in Carmen's face. "But what if it's the only way to save Flynn? Is that reason enough to try?"

Carmen frowned, but nodded, head dipped, ashamed. Of course, Flynn was worth it.

Roman gestured with the beam towards the stairs, and together, they ascended.

When Shadows Creep

...

Finnigan

Finnigan moved slowly down the hall, head cocked, listening. Something had passed through the corridor outside of his room only moments before, a strange, exuberant scratching that had traveled quickly. Too quickly for Finnigan to look up from his book to see.

He had dashed out into the corridor in socked feet, sliding slightly as he stopped, but nothing was there. He knew he had heard it, though, and that's all that mattered to him. He'd hunt it down, trap it, catch it, whatever needed to be done and he would get it the Hell out of Caldwell Manor.

Whatever it had done to Flynn, whatever it *was doing* to Flynn, was unforgivable. Flynn had returned a shell of his former self. Damaged. Something in Finnigan had twisted once he had discovered what had happened to Flynn. There was a small part of him that lurked below the surface, blaming him for letting Flynn leave. He had never felt guilt like this before. He believed deeply that healing the hurt was the only way to make it up to him, to show him that his apology was more than just words. That they reflected the actions he'd take to bring Flynn back into good health.

A door slammed up ahead.

He ran the last few yards and stood outside a glass-paned French door with intricately frosted panels. The inside of the room was bathed in sunlight, even though it had been the dark of night when he left his room. A shadow passed between the light and the door, a ripple across the glass. Finnigan squared his shoulders and flung the door wide, prepared to capture the intruder unaware.

The room beyond was dark. Only a closet, a mop bucket, and broom were leaning haphazard against a shelf full of ancient cleaning supplies.

Finnigan frowned and looked behind the door, which was now plain and brown and scuffed. He pulled the small chain connected to the bare bulb above his head and it weakly illuminated the space.

Finnigan backed away from the storage closet and softly shut the door behind him. Every other door in the hallway cascaded closed in a pulsing rhythm that started at his end of the corridor and worked its way to the very end. Finnigan yelped and pressed against the wall, holding his hands to his ears against the avalanche of noise. It was a good fifteen or sixteen doors, considering the current state of the wing.

"You want to make this difficult, do you?!" Finnigan yelled. He released his knife into his palm and held it lowered at his side, just in case he finally did meet the creature that was using the Manor against them.

When Shadows Creep

Finnigan headed toward the stairs, the only point of exit from this end of the Manor. The light from the chandelier's crystals pooled there, and patterns of light moved along the walls in ripples and arcs as if a heavy wind blew through the great hall and disturbed the sparkling glass.

The sconces on the walls behind him were snuffed out suddenly. As he passed door after door in his haste, more and more of the lights began to blink out, one after the other after the other.

Finnigan's heart pounded in his chest, his pace increased, and the panic fluttered low in his belly.

This isn't happening.

He wanted to stop. Wanted to turn and face the Dark, to fight the faceless foe. But a good and large part of him was certain that oblivion waited in the deepness of it, and that was what he must outrun.

He slid to a stop at the top of the landing. The railing had become a neat half circle with no exit. The massive sweeping staircase had completely disappeared. He leaned as far over the railing as he could, took in the patterned tiles below, glossy with newness.

"Carmen!" Finnigan yelled, from deep in his gut, as loud as he could. He hoped that the Manor would pull the sound through, bounce it along as it did, and reach wherever Carmen was holed up.

He turned so that his back was pressed to the firm brass of the railing, solid against him, warm and reassuring, and watched as the last two lights clicked off.

. . .

Caden

Caden had already lost Flynn.

He'd slipped around a corner, hand dragging along the wall at the top of the wainscoting. Whether for support or guidance, Caden couldn't quite figure, and then Flynn was gone.

The hallway in both directions empty, free of adjoining doors, and Flynn completely evaporated. Caden wished he knew what had gotten into Flynn. He never used to be this damned defiant, not before he left.

Not at all.

And now? It was a constant walk across glass, as Caden tried to ensure he both protected Flynn and gave him his space. It felt like weeks ago that he had shown up at the Freemont House to convince Flynn to return, not twenty-four hours. Then again, he thought, they were dealing with something that seemed to be able to change how they perceived time and how it passed.

Maybe days had gone by.

When Shadows Creep

Caden shuddered at the thought. Living for eternity was one thing, but it was the sense of time passing that kept them anchored and sane. Take that away, and they'd all quickly lose their minds.

Caden paced down the hallway, eyes and ears open for any sign of Flynn. Or anyone, really. The Manor was eerily quiet considering four people were roaming the halls in a state of nervous anxiety.

He considered calling out. Maybe Flynn had gotten twisted into another room by accident and he needed to hear Caden's voice to sort his way out. But something stilled his voice before it could leave his throat. Something was wrong.

A draft blew across the back of his neck followed by the sensation that something was moving over his head. There was a rustle and a glimpse of movement in his peripheral vision.

Caden's head snapped up, and that was when he saw it. A trapdoor in the ceiling, the chain swinging mere inches above his head. Mere seconds before he would have sworn nothing was there.

Caden stepped back and tugged on the chain, gently at first, but it wouldn't give. He put his full weight behind the next pull, and the door popped free. An extendable ladder shot over his head in a cloud of dust to rest half-opened four feet from the ground.

Caden narrowed his eyes. There'd never been more than two floors, regardless of the sprawling spread of the wings and rooms and halls of the Manor. History didn't lend itself to building upward; this building only went outward. It concerned him that there was more to the Manor than had been revealed to him in many, many years.

Cold air wafted down from above. He debated leaving, of finding Carmen, Finnigan, anyone who could watch his back and ensure he wasn't trapped in the dust and the dark of this new third floor. Maybe it was uninsulated and that explained the temperature change. Caden squinted up and attempted to see if any light, however faint, came through. *Or.*

Or—and this made Caden's heart skip a beat—or maybe there had been a point in time when the Manor had three floors. And that point in time was in the winter, who knew what year or in what version of this universe. That would certainly make that floor several degrees colder than anywhere else in the Manor. Somewhere that a person could freeze to death. Or where something that lived for the cold and the dark could safely stay hidden, above the warmth and the relative safety of the House.

When a place in this version of earth was in proximity with the undercurrent, the flow of the multiverse became strong, affected everything around it. This was a world where every outcome was simultaneously possible, and impossible,

When Shadows Creep

and the Guardians experienced the ever changing parameters as a matter of course. The Manor shifted, this was normal. It became versions and variants of every possible version of itself. Patterns could be understood, tracked. It stuck to the basic seasons of this world, at least on the outside, as outlined by this timeline. But inside, a room may only exist in one winter of one universe.

It explained their obsession with windows. Like a magnetic North, the windows always beckoned them. Sometimes it was the only clue to where, or *when*, the Manor wanted to be. Sometimes, you didn't want to see. Sometimes that universe of that room was a horrible place.

Roman would close off those rooms, instruct the Manor to never let that shift move into pattern ever again, and that horror would be locked away.

Caden hated the multiverse theory. It made his brain turn to mush when he thought about every possible result of every possible choice generating a split into another universe.

He swallowed hard as he continued to stare up at the gaping dark of the access to the third floor. He could hear voices up there, a quiet discussion, hushed in the dark. He craned his neck, placed one foot on the ladder trying to get closer to the conversation without committing to climbing up into that darkened place.

Caden rose one more step. His height put his head much closer to the opening than he was comfortable with. His imagination overran his brain with thoughts of hands, pale, deathly, reaching from above and grabbing him by his hair; dragging him up and away to where none of the others could find him.

It was so cold. His breath hung about his face in wisps every time he exhaled, shallow because he held his breath with the need to hear what the voices were saying.

"Carmen!" Finnigan's shout echoed in another wing over, a reverberation through the Manor, amplified. Caden froze.

The desperation in Finnigan's voice was evident. The panicked quaver in his voice shook Caden to his core. He took one last look at the darkness above his head and made a quick decision. Finnigan first.

He leapt to the ground and took off as fast as he could toward the far-off glow of the central hall, pink against the dark of the wood paneling in the corridor. Caden kicked off his slippers as they slowed his desperate race for Finnigan. He left them scattered near a large potted plant that covered the exit from the wing he was coming from to the central hub.

He pushed through the dark, overgrown palm leaves and came face to face with a brass railing that prevented him from any further progress. Caden stared across the expanse of the great hall to where Finnigan clung to the outside of a railing. Caden was trapped on his half of the building by a small and rounded curve of balcony.

"Finnigan! Hold on!"

Finnigan's feet dangled the stretch to the first floor well over a distance of twenty feet below. He had his arms locked between the gleaming copper balustrades, holding on for dear life.

"What do you think I'm doing?" Finnigan's panicked shriek came back. He kicked, trying to scramble for purchase.

Caden assessed the situation, his view obscured by the massive chandelier that dominated the space. The four thousand crystals that hung wired from its wrought iron arms shimmered in a breeze that Caden didn't feel, and scattered light in every direction. Except for the hall where Finnigan's balcony bridged out from the wall. That hall was darkness, black as black. No light passed beyond the black and white checked tile of the balcony.

Eighteen feet separated Caden from Finnigan. Twenty-four feet from the edge of Finnigan's balcony to the floor. The math was too grand, the room too great to allow for any easy solution.

"I'm coming for you, Finnigan!" Caden shouted.

Chapter Ten

Carmen

Roman and Carmen stepped lightly along the gray and rotten floorboards. Every step made an ominous creak and they would pause, breath held, in case they fell clear through to the floors below. There was no telling where the rest of this Manor was, but it was far too cold. Their breath drifted in every sweep of his flashlight. The wind howled and battered the outside of the House, whistling through invisible cracks in the shingles.

"Have you ever been here before?" Carmen whispered, a hand tentatively at Roman's elbow to avoid separation in the dark.

Roman responded with a quiet noise, too quiet to hear over the rush of the wind and sleet. He paused and his flashlight beam followed a clear trail through the thick dust that coated the ground beneath their feet.

Something had been dragged, or slid, through the dust. The trail stretched from one distant end, far outside the reach of the flashlight, toward the direction they had been walking.

Carmen had begun to shiver in the cold of the attic, dressed for an evening indoors, perched by a fire. Not for a wander through a room in the thick of a winter storm.

"I don't think the Manor created this room," Roman murmured.

His light pointed at the ceiling far, far above their heads. A cathedral ceiling with massive beams crossed over their heads. It denoted a building far larger than any version of the Manor they'd ever seen. A sharp snap of panic rippled through Carmen. "Then what did?"

If something happened to the Manor, if it was taken over, dried up, if they had to leave, where would they go? They'd be adrift in a world they had no right being in. They protected the humans from contact with the undercurrent that flowed between the multiverses. If they had to abandon it, how could they live with the loss?

Carmen began to hyperventilate.

Roman turned and put a hand on Carmen's shoulder and a finger to his own lips. The light from the flashlight highlighted the angles and planes of his face in a grotesque mask, the way children would tell stories around the campfire. Carmen silenced, bottom lip bitten between teeth that chattered.

A rush of icy air billowed around them in a swirl of dust and ice crystals. Sharp needles pricked at their face and hands, and they gasped against the burst. Roman took one last look off into the distance where the trail had led and shook his head. "We can't get lost up here, we'll die of exposure. Which sounds insane, even as I say it, indoors as we are, but we must get down and find the others. I have to speak to Flynn about what happened at Freemont House."

Carmen nodded in agreement and turned back toward where the stairwell had opened up out of the floor. They had left the door propped open to give them a sightline to the warm glow below. But solid darkness greeted Carmen in every direction. Carmen stepped back, bumped into Roman, who reached out a steadying hand.

"It's okay Carmen. We'll find it. We'll find the way back out. This is still our House. We still have a degree of control over this space, even if the Manor didn't create it, just focus. Focus on the central staircase, focus on your memory of the chandelier. Think about the smell of the room, how it always has a slight spice to it like newly fallen leaves. Remember the warmth of the kitchen when I found you earlier. Think hard, Carmen. Together we'll return to the rest of the Manor. Think about it now,"

Carmen could feel Roman's breath, the only warmth in this diseased off-shoot of the Manor and concentrated on the sensation, trying to mirror the memory on top of the feeling, a combination designed to concentrate the request of the House.

A flicker of thought towards the deck where Carmen had sat, mostly relaxed, only a few hours before. The thought coalesced on the memory of Caden staring across the fields at the deer. Carmen exhaled. The memories almost burned away the brisk air of the attic, almost completely submerged Carmen in the warmth of the undercurrent. A rumble began in the distance and coursed across the floor, shook the floorboards beneath their feet, and they staggered.

Light came from a newly opened hole in the floor, and through it, a cry. "Carmen!"

The Manor flung it at them as loud as if it had come from beside them, and Carmen's heart twisted with the fear at the core of it. They hurried toward the hole, a trapdoor open, a ladder extended below. Carmen went first, using only two of the eight steps, hands sliding down the metal handrail. Roman mirrored the action and made it down without trauma.

"Finnigan! Hold on!" Caden's voice came to them raised and panicked from the end of the hall. It was a sure sign that something had gone horribly wrong with Finnigan. Caden rarely raised his voice.

Together, Carmen and Roman took off toward the source of the screams, feet pounding in unison, matched in their long-legged strides.

Carmen had a split second to realize that this hallway had become free of any doors, before almost tripping over a discarded pair of slippers. They were scarlet against the hardwood. Caden's.

Roman hauled Carmen up from the half-stumble as they carried onward. They slammed into a balcony railing at the end, unable to continue around the edge of the room.

Roman's eyes reflected the confusion Carmen felt. The absence of the staircase spoke louder about the state of the Manor than they'd realized. It had been an anchor for the Manor for too many years now, the twist of the rooms around reality had been centered on this spot for so long, they'd almost forgotten it wasn't permanent.

Carmen gaped at the pattern of tiles below, caught up in the broad, open expanse of floor. Roman grabbed Carmen's arm, hand extended at the scene in front of them.

Finnigan dangled from the opposing balcony, as his legs swung in the wide and empty space. Caden was perched on an arm of the chandelier. He slowly and methodically made his way through the swinging crystals as the entire fixture shuddered with each motion.

"It's going to come down. There's no way he can stay up there." Roman sounded detached from the situation. He had assessed, processed, and issued his opinion, without the slightest note of concern.

When Shadows Creep

"What exactly is your plan, Caden?" Roman boomed across the empty space as Caden monkeyed to a lower level of wrought iron, bars as thick as his wrist.

A shifting tinkle of sound washed over them as the great beast of a fixture tipped in slow motion toward them. Caden had crossed the counter balance, and the whole of it swung toward where Carmen anxiously stood.

Caden shook his head. Until that very moment, he didn't know Roman had returned. Carmen silently begged him to focus on his task at hand, at where Finnigan hung. He had three more feet to move, but the chandelier was a large and elegant raindrop shape, far larger at the bottom than the top. He'd run out of hand holds soon.

Caden was perched precariously at the midway point of the arm he knelt on, hands wrapped around the bar so tightly Carmen could see the white of his knuckles. If he moved any farther forward, the entire piece would cantilever. He'd be pitched down to the marble below. Or—and this was the constant panicked thought at the base of Carmen's brain – the thick chain that held the fixture to the ceiling would give way. It would disconnect from the beam over his head, and he'd be no better than dead.

...

Finnigan

The thought of a solo plummet was only a notch better than the thought of a fall surrounded by shards of glass. Glass that would shatter and pierce him a thousand times over when he landed in them.

What *was* Caden's plan?

At that moment Finnigan slipped. He'd had his arms through the bars, was holding on tightly to his elbows with his hands. He'd been afraid to adjust his grip to the balustrades, a sure way to slip to the floor. But a shift in his weight caused himself to undo all the progress he'd made.

"Finnigan!" Caden's voice rang out.

Now, Finnigan was dangling by one hand. He'd managed to catch a rod at the absolute last moment. He twisted with the momentum and groaned as his shoulder wrenched beyond where it should ever go, bearing all his weight. Swear words spewed from his lips, and he blinked back tears of pain.

"I'm just going to take my chances, Caden, go back, don't risk it! I'm just going to drop. It hurts too much!" Finnigan shouted over his shoulder. He already knew he had dislocated it.

He bit his tongue, tried to keep his brain focused on this pain. It was a different pain, one that wouldn't necessarily make him pass out and drop to the floor below. If anything, he'd have to remain conscious if he did fall, if only to control it.

Maybe he could tuck and roll.

The chandelier jangled above him, Caden swaying. It appeared he'd taken another hesitant inch toward him. The whole chandelier began to swing again slowly with the motion, the chain creaking. Caden's hands lifted from the cross bar as he balanced on his knees.

"Life isn't a God damn action movie, you idiot!" Finnigan yelled, half to himself, half to Caden. He shifted another few cautious inches forward.

"Shut up, Finnigan. You're as bad as your brother," Caden retorted. "I'll be able to sense the exact moment the chandelier shifts. When it does, I'll use the momentum to launch myself towards the railing."

Finnigan's thoughts were scattered. At any second he could fall to his death. Caden had the reach, he had the strength. He just needed a little momentum to get himself in the right direction.

Sweat poured into his eyes, he tried to wipe it away with his shoulder and his hand began to slide.

"Caden, please, just stop, stay there, we'll find a way to get you, we'll find a ladder or something!" Carmen called across the gap.

The distance looked far larger now than it had, and Caden looked miles away.

The thought scrambled across Finnigan's mind that just maybe it had stretched wider in the interim.

Anything was possible right now, with the Manor in disarray.

A hysterical screech wrenched from the ceiling above Finnigan's head. Everyone's heads snapped up, looking for the source of the ear-splitting sound.

A smear of inky darkness wrapped around the chain. One of the links had split, separated at a weak spot, and the metal was stretching. The darkness moved, sliding farther down the chain.

Carmen and Roman gaped, but Finnigan couldn't focus on anything except his weakening grip. Then his fingers slipped.

Caden dove toward him as a loud peal of hysterical laughter bounced around the space. It skittered away along the ceiling and through the darkened hallway. The sconces sputtered back to life, and Caden dove toward Finnigan's freefall.

Upon reflection later that night, no one could quite trace exactly what happened. As far as anyone could tell, the Manor had seemed to finally shake itself free of the hold the intruder had on its control of time and space. It had reverted to its original state. The winding marble staircase reasserted itself from thin air, a gliding circular twist up from the floor below.

If Finnigan had fallen, after he dropped, he would have simply slid down several steps. His knees would have crumpled onto the stairs below where he dangled and all would have been well.

Caden however had leapt. The momentum of Caden's body weight had crushed both of them against the risers and knocked the air from them. Finnigan's scream from the pressure on his wrenched shoulder echoed in the quiet astonishment of the Guardians.

Caden had rolled off of Finnigan, apologizing profusely. Finnigan steeled his breath to a point where he could curse Caden's name. "Never. Ever. Save me again," Finnigan wheezed.

. . .

Caden

They sat scattered amongst Carmen's office at a loss for words.

Carmen had returned Finnigan's arm to where it belonged, though only with help from Caden holding him steady, and a whisky bottle to dull his pain. Finnigan now sat dazed in the corner of the couch by the fire. He held the bottle in his lap, knuckles white around the glass.

Caden was perched on the edge of the wide mahogany desk. His fingers dug into the edge of the desk as if it were the only thing that kept him tethered to the ground.

Roman and Carmen sat in the matching floral armchairs that faced each other. Their hands and faces were now clean from the smudges of dust and dirt that had streaked across their skin while they'd attempted to explore the attic. An antique chessboard, absent of its pieces, sat between them.

Carmen's dark eyes caught Caden's stare, "And you're sure you have no idea where Flynn has gone?"

A raised eyebrow.

Caden rolled his eyes. "If I had an idea, I'd be looking for him, now wouldn't I?"

Carmen huffed.

"Listen, children, this gets us nowhere," Roman chided.

"Maybe. Maybe he, maybe he squished him," Finnigan's slurred laughter came from the couch.

Three sets of eyes rolled.

Roman re-crossed his legs and turned toward Caden. He leaned over the armrest, segregating Finnigan from the conversation. "Where exactly did he say he thought he was when he woke up? You mentioned he had no idea he'd been asleep all day, unconscious really, but you mentioned he dreamt of the garden?"

Caden nodded, crossing his arms tight across his chest. "He said he'd been out in the garden for the afternoon, that it was the most beautiful night, and then he reached into his pocket."

Caden stared at his hand for a moment and recreated the gesture he'd witnessed Flynn perform. He pulled his hand away from his chest and opened it as if he'd expected something to be there. He frowned and repeated the action once more.

"He had something, when he woke up, didn't he?" Roman surmised and rose from his chair.

Caden wrinkled his nose and shrugged, but after a moment nodded in agreement.

"Knowing Flynn, would he attempt to recreate where he'd been before he awoke, to attempt to continue what he'd been doing? A task of some sort?" Carmen asked, and looked pointedly at Roman.

Roman considered for a moment. He sat back in the chair and rested his chin in his hand. The clock ticked onward and a log in the fire shifted, sending sparks a-flutter behind the screen. The popping sound startled them all except for Finnigan who seemed unfazed and took another swig from his brown bottle.

"Well?" Carmen asked, annoyance clear in voice and tone.

Roman cleared his throat. "This is likely, yes. There's a good chance that is where he is right now, out in the garden.

But it is also likely that if we are all to leave the Manor in search of him we wouldn't be able to get back in."

Caden paled at these words.

Roman continued. "We've already seen that whatever followed Flynn— whatever's *afflicting* him— can alter the Manor at its whim. It's using the power of the undercurrent against us. It's generating alternate shifts faster than I've ever seen a House do. The incident with the stairs, and the room above the second floor, attic or whatever it is, can only be the beginning." Roman punctuated the end of his statement by leaning forward over his long legs and resting his elbows on his knees, head in his hands.

"You guys were up there?" Caden asked quietly. He had been distraught over the thought that Flynn may have escaped up into that space. He thought because he had been far too scared to climb that ladder, that somehow Flynn was trapped up there, unable to return.

Carmen reached out a hand and patted him on the knee. "Don't worry, there was no one up there besides us, it had that absence to it. Like we were the only ones around with heartbeats, you know what I mean?"

"But you didn't explore it all, you didn't check every corner?" Caden said.

"Well, no," Carmen gestured helplessly at Finnigan, who had fallen asleep with his cheek pressed against the armrest. He cradled his injured arm stiff across his body, the bottle now resting on the floor.

"So our options are outside, where we may be trapped against our will, unable to get back inside. Or, up to the attic which only exists when it wants to. And could also trap us against our will, unable to get out," Caden said, exasperated. He stared up at the ceiling as if the answers might be engraved in the plaster.

"Caden, you realize that statement is true for anywhere in the Manor right? We could be trapped in this office and just not realize it yet," Carmen said. Caden lowered his eyes to stare at Carmen, and the truth of the matter rang in his ears.

They weren't safe here. They weren't safe anywhere.

They couldn't leave, they couldn't stay. They couldn't find it to fight it, they couldn't speak with it to reason with it.

They didn't even know what *it* was.

"You guys saw it, right? You saw it breaking the chain? That dark...?" Caden looked around and for a moment assumed he'd imagined it. Anything, in the heat of the moment, could be imagined. But everyone nodded in response.

"Any idea what it is? Was? Roman, have you seen anything like it before?" Carmen's voice trembled with the question, and Roman shook his head in a slow arc.

They were all on edge. They'd had their choices stripped away from them and it was more than any of them could take. Roman, their rock, their leader, looked as shaken as the rest of them.

"I shouldn't have left. I could have done something if I'd just been here," Roman said.

"Don't blame yourself Roman. You already said you thought you were losing Flynn to his distance from the undercurrent. Not some evil that stripped him down to nothing. You had no way of knowing."

As Carmen finished trying to reassure Roman, he slammed his fist down onto the chessboard and sent it flying.

Finnigan roused from his slumber and sat up, hair matted to one side of his face, and looked around at their tense expressions.

"So we split up?" Finnigan's voice was raw from pain and the alcohol and he grimaced as he took a sip from the water glass by his head.

"We can't split up, Finnigan. That's precisely what led us to the mess we're in now. No one should be alone right now. Hell, we clearly can't even be in pairs after the events of this evening. We have to stick together." Roman spoke in a firm, even tone. It was a decree more than a suggestion.

Finnigan settled back into a supine position, his good arm thrown up over his eyes, body turned toward the back of the couch.

When Shadows Creep

Caden assumed he'd gone back to sleep until he asked, "Why don't we just ask the Manor to show us? It's been losing its mind fairly frequently since *whatever it is* arrived, but only when and where bad things are going down. Can't it just lead us to where the thing is?"

Roman fixed his eerie green gaze on Finnigan's prone form, the fire reflecting in his eyes. It turned them strange and cat-like, as otherworldly as their roots in this world.

"I should have thought of that," Roman gaped.

Carmen shrugged and spoke up,

"Well, we ask it to do things normally, to shift us where we need to be or to create where we need to go. We did it earlier when the attic swallowed us up. Why not ask it to bend toward a person, to shift us to where they are?"

Roman thoughtfully drummed his fingers on the arm of the chair. "We could find Flynn that way too, no?" Caden asked.

A ripple of excitement rounded the room. The office fluttered through variants of vibrant, red patterned wallpaper adorned in roses and poppies and cardinals.

Roman's head snapped up and he smiled. "I think the Manor agrees with us."

Chapter Eleven

The Dark

It hummed to itself as It spiraled its way through the darkened hallways. The sconces flickered when it passed too close.

It was good that the light reacted to the Dark in such a way. The light was alive, in its own way. It understood what the Dark represented.

Now that Flynn had its gift, had a piece of itself, hardened and shiny and dark, sitting in his pocket, it always knew where he was. Always knew how he felt. It rested against Flynn's heart, exactly where it needed to be.

Now it could worry about the rest of them, drive them slowly mad until It drove them out. It would have the Manor and all its power to itself. It would have Flynn.

It could get into the cracks.

Spread throughout the multiverse.

When Shadows Creep

Exist within every rendition of every version of the world.

Oh, the beauty of it.

And the Dark would rise up. It wouldn't have to stay hiding in the deep of the waters anymore.

A cackle broke free from it as it slipped between the studs in the wall. It slid past the desiccated corpse of a mouse, along with the thousands of clumps of dust and debris that had collected in the walls.

It climbed, and It absorbed the thoughts of the Manor as It flickered by.

Good luck, House. You cannot remove me so easy.

The route It had planned twisted, a sudden stop in a dead end. The Dark was gleeful. It could take anything this rumbling pile of wood and masonry threw at it.

The Dark concentrated. A pipe opened in the wall and the way through to the attic was clear.

It slipped into the freezing cold air and the absolute dark of the room in which it had tested its newfound abilities.

Yes.

It remembered this place, from centuries before. There had been a time when it was worshipped by men, called upon, and the Dark had crawled from the sea, to inhabit places just like this.

In the mountains, in the cold, in the deep darkness of the wilds.

Oh, the wilds.

It missed the electric bloody survival of it all. You killed or were killed, you ate and drank your enemies and absorbed them into your core, or you didn't survive at all.

The Dark had grown then, so large, in the hearts of man and beast alike. It moved from victim to victim, feeding on the inherent evil in the violent nature of the land.

But the world became a brighter place. It sucked the shadows out of the lands, lightened every corner.

Rules. Laws.

Bloody laws. Bloody people…

And then this place had burned to the ground. In the light of the world, people realized something was wrong.

It hissed at the thought and fanned itself out toward the massive oak beam that supported the ceiling of this winter place. It clung by a shred of darkness and hung, heavy and cloying.

It was darker than the dark in this lightless place, and It settled in to absorb. To rest. To learn. The Manor gave a shudder, a thud of air around the Dark, as it attempted to collapse the space. But the Darkness resisted.

This time, It would go nowhere against its will.

When Shadows Creep

. . .

Flynn

Flynn had made it as far as the monstrous stone guardians at the end of the driveway. He stared at the great carved winged beasts. They had the bodies of lions but the heads of massive stags, their antlers so large and outspread that they almost entwined in an arch over the road. Their wings, outspread, feathered, a full fifteen feet from tip to tip as the lion bodies reared upward.

They were horrible. Just looking at the strange beasts made Flynn's skin crawl. He'd never seen anything like them in his years at the Manor.

But the Manor had been doing all sorts of strange things Flynn had never seen before. Even out here, on the outskirts of the real world and the infinite universe. It had been strange enough that the driveway had flickered between cobblestone, tar, concrete, and dirt as Flynn walked. But to have these things appear the moment he had turned back to peer at the Manor was more than Flynn bargained for.

He stood on the edge, between the property and the municipal road. This road, unaffected by proximity to the undercurrent, glimmered in the light as it winded off through the trees in both directions. It had rained at some point and the tarmac glistened in the early dawn light that had only just crested the hill of farmland that faced the

Manor. Everything was an absurd shade of pink and made the surrounding trees appear alien.

He touched his breast pocket tentatively, the firm weight of the stone-like egg warm against his chest.

The further he moved from the Manor, the warmer it had become, and was now just a few degrees below uncomfortable. At the moment, though, the heat was welcome.

He'd left the Manor as he'd left his room, in socked feet and only a pullover over his t-shirt and pants. Flynn's socks were drenched and his feet ached with cold.

Flynn wasn't aware of how he had gotten out here. One moment he'd spoke with Caden, and the next he realized he was halfway down the twisting driveway. He had an almost painful desire to put as much distance between himself and the others as possible.

"They can't know about you," he patted his pocket and felt a responding tremor from the *thing*.

Flynn settled on the edge of the stone plinth that held one of the stone monsters, feet pulled up and one arm wrapped around his knees. They wouldn't be able to see him here, protected by the great sweep of wings behind the beast.

He reached down the collar of his pullover and into the pocket of his shirt and pulled out the object the raven had given him.

When Shadows Creep

Caden had told him it was only a dream, but he didn't quite believe it. How else could this thing be here? You couldn't dream things into existence; that wasn't how the world worked. Things either already existed, or they didn't.

Guardians' dreams were no different than humans. Dreams were just an unconscious slide between the cracks of realities. You became a witness to things that would never happen, or exist in your home world. Things that had happened a thousand different ways, a thousand times over, in all the others.

And why not?

Dreams weren't there to hurt you.

So that was the rule. Nothing in, nothing out.

But here this thing was.

Caden lied to you.

The hiss of words seemed to ooze from the smooth surface of the egg, black as black. Not a single ray of the rising sun reflected from its surface. Flynn almost dropped it into the muddy grass beneath his feet but caught it at the last moment with scrabbling fingertips. He tucked it into the crook of his elbow and pushed his hand through his long white hair. He tucked it neatly onto its correct side before he scratched lightly at the shorter, mahogany side of his scalp. He stared down at the thing, wondered if it would speak to him again.

"You know things, don't you?"

His query was quiet in the still morning air.

The sun broke free of the horizon. It dropped the earth away as heavy as a mantle and rose, red and wet from the broken farmland in front of Flynn. He squinted up at the bright rays, warm on his chilled face and his frost-kissed nose. He could feel his skin melting with the warmth, the ache in his muscles shifted to the tingle of revival.

Flynn's face broke into a smile and he closed his eyes.

The egg rattled with warning, and the sudden rattle-snake-like sound sent a shock through his limbs. He looked down at it, concerned. Golden light was thrown across his arms and chest, and he frowned. He slipped the egg into the pouch of his pullover and it quieted, his hand gentle where it rested.

"You see the world the same as I do, don't you? The light is so bright, sometimes it's better to just turn it all off. Whatever happened to me, when you revealed yourself, when it changed me, my eyes, my way of looking at the world, it's given me something I didn't know I needed before. A way to see the dark in the world. In people. Everything that crawls just below the surface where it thinks it is hidden. But I see it, oh I do."

Flynn sighed, more to himself than to the egg, but his grip tightened. "At least you don't lie about hiding in the dark. You are the Dark and nothing else, nothing less. I should be thankful for that."

When Shadows Creep

Flynn began to hum, a tune that had never known words. A haunted sound.

Unbeknownst to him, this was not a tune he'd ever heard. It was not a tune he'd ever known. It was not a tune he'd made up himself. It wasn't a comfort for when he was alone, to keep himself company after he ran so far from the Manor so many years ago.

No.

But the tune was a favorite of the Dark, and so it played through Flynn.

...

Carmen

The four remaining Guardians left Carmen's office and moved to the room with the staircase. Finnigan side-eyed the risers and was voracious in his multiple decrees that there was "*no way on this or any other plane of existence*" that he'd be climbing those stairs.

They sat beneath the chandelier, each one with their back turned towards a compass direction, as the empty halls stretched behind them.

Caden had vehemently argued about this position, but Carmen pointed out that the Manor had already corrected the damage done by the dark smear, and it should now perfectly safe.

But Caden had wiggled back from his proposed position so many times in defiance of this advice that Carmen had ceased the eye rolling and sighs, and has just accepted that it was far too soon for Caden to be back in this room.

They all held hands. Finnigan fidgeted in Caden's grasp. The liquor he'd drank as pain relief earlier had worn off, it showed on his face. Roman had sat, stone still, eyes closed, chin pointed toward the floor without a single waver in his posture for close to twenty minutes.

Occasionally, the lights would flicker, dim, brighten, change in shape and style. The other details of the wings and room remained the same. Carmen looked around with wide eyes. It was as if Roman communicated with the Manor in actual conversation, in a language that only he and it could understand.

The room buzzed with the sound of the changes in electricity, the Guardians completely silent except for the occasional gasp of frustrated pain from Finnigan.

The chandelier and every bulb in every sconce flared up making it too bright to see. Every room was a stark contrast against the light, every crack and every seam outlined in a harsh silver edged light. Every shadow disappeared; no corner for anything to lurk in remained. They winced against the light, eyes closed against the brightness.

Everything was exposed to the light, like under a flipped-over stone.

When Shadows Creep

The Manor would find it, of course, it would. It would drag the Dark kicking and screaming into the light. And then they'd find a way to stop it.

Every window and every door in every wing of the Manor flung open, a resounding crash that echoed throughout the building. The brisk autumn air rushed through, and scattered papers from one room to the next. A billowing collection of everything lightweight and unconstrained began to funnel by. Despite all this, nothing swam to the surface and revealed itself. No angry cry howled from any room or shrieked against the indignity of its removal.

Carmen looked at Roman, brow furrowed. He'd gone into the undercurrent, his face slack. It was easier, Carmen guessed, for him to speak with the entirety of the Manor, rather than just its current form.

The windows slammed shut, and the last swirl of papers settled about them and across their laps. Caden muttered something about a cleanup, which Carmen guessed he believed fell to him.

"Any luck?" Finnigan's voice was quiet and scared against the echo of silence.

This had been their only idea and if it went the wrong way, well, what could they do besides wait for the Dark to reveal its plan? It was likely too late to do anything to fix it before it ruined this world and possibly all the others.

Roman blinked hard once, twice, and released their hands. Finnigan's bad arm dropped into his lap, and he rubbed his shoulder tiredly. Roman focused on Carmen, a tired half-smile quirked the corner of his lips. He nodded.

"Flynn's on the outskirts. The sun just came up. The Dark doesn't like the light."

"Go figure," Carmen muttered and rose to standing.

Caden reached down and heaved Finnigan up to his feet. Finnigan grimaced and grunted. He covered the sound with a cough when Roman threw a glare his way.

...

Caden

Caden paused in front of the hall that led to the front of the house. They were headed toward the doors that he and Carmen had so desperately tried to get into not so long ago. And now they were going to force their way back out, find Flynn, and find out precisely what Flynn believed was going on. Hopefully he was still in control of himself enough for them to get answers.

As wayward as Flynn had been over the past few years, leaving the Manor, building his own House out of that abandoned hillside bed and breakfast, and actively choosing to live in a place where something lurked outside of his control, at the core of it all, Caden hoped he was still regular old

138

When Shadows Creep

Flynn. That abstract and gentle soul. The love of the moon, his restlessness and wanderlust that increased through the darkness of the night. It had always peaked around two in the morning, always. Caden used to find him perched on the rooftop of the Manor, boots steady against the slate as he gazed up at the stars.

And now what?

The Darkness had found him and it assaulted that wistful twist to his heart and used it against him.

For what?

It made Caden's blood boil. He was glad for Carmen's gentle touch. This situation would no doubt escalate outside of Caden's control otherwise.

Caden zipped his jacket over his long sleeved collarless tee, the brilliant red clashing with the orange hue of the hallway. Carmen squeezed his hand while passing by, and slipped on a similar coat of cut and fabric. Carmen's coat, however, was in a color akin to the autumn sky outside. Roman donned green, and Finnigan was in his yellow that Carmen helped him slip on, his arm dangling helplessly at his side.

Caden shook his head. They looked more like a parade of kindergarteners or a flock of pretty birds than a team of centuries-old Guardians deeded with protecting the multiverse.

Roman paused at the door, his hand on the knob, and rested his forehead against the slate gray of the wood and muttered under his breath. Moments later, Roman turned, one hand still splayed against the wood. He nodded at them all. "Ready?"

...

Flynn

A door slammed somewhere far off like a gunshot crack in the quiet countryside. He spied a raven as it coasted overhead, soaring on the updrafts from the heat of the road.

Flynn waited patiently, wondered if it was the same bird from the garden.

Your dream, he thought and then shook his head as if he could knock the thought clear from his brain.

It was real, he retaliated, but shortly realized there was no use in arguing with himself. Or the sound of Caden in his head.

"I shouldn't be out here. Not alone. It's not safe. Not safe at all," Flynn muttered, shrinking against the stone.

He felt ill. His stomach rolled with conflicting thoughts and images. He gently stroked the stone, each touch of his hand against the cool surface cemented his belief that everything was fine. He was right, Caden was wrong, and the Dark meant him no harm. It protected him and kept him safe.

But when he removed his hands from his pocket and rubbed them together to warm them with the friction of the motion, it all flooded back; the terror of the dark, the way it crept along the edges of his brain, pried away at the seams, and looked for a way in.

The way that Carmen had looked at him after inspecting his back, the concern and the fear behind eyes that tried their hardest to be calm and relaxed. Eyes that tried to keep him from worrying.

The absence of the stone in his hand was like being dropped into a sea of panic and discontent. His subconscious was screaming at him to grab anything to hold on to as wave after wave of fear rushed over him in sheer nerve-shredding blackness. Along with this flood, there was a mistrust— a sensation Flynn struggled to fight— of his housemates, his fellow Guardians. Deep in his gut, he knew, they were not the problem. They were more than just his friends.

You didn't exist in tandem with others for centuries and *not* build a bond stronger than any malicious force, and yet…

And yet.

They want the stone. They want to take it from you. They want to destroy it. You can't let them.

Flynn struggled against the thought and then relaxed. He had reached for the stone, had taken a deep shudder of a breath, and calmed. It was so much nicer to just exist.

He floated along on the icy air, curled against the stone lion feet with paws the size of cannonballs, his mind adrift. A tugging at the base of his spine. The undercurrent, hesitant and feather-light, tickled against his brain. It encouraged him to drift into the oblivion.

He hadn't been exposed— not directly— to the undercurrent before. But then his head spun, and he felt himself tip head over heels. An endless tumbling, down, down, though his feet never left the ground. As suddenly as it began, the sensation stopped and his stomach righted, pulled by a magnetic north he felt deep within his soul. He stood trance-like and stared at the Manor in his mind.

It was different here. The Manor had lost its glow here. In this version of the world it was just a building. A large one, though barely distinguishable from an oversized barn. It was made with heavy wood, heavy beams, and it was perched on a hillside surrounded by waist-deep snow. The wind howled by and buried everything in an icy tomb.

Darkness surrounded everything. The white snow shimmered in moonlight that fought its way through heavy clouds in bursts and gasps; a dying light in the ever-dark of this reality. Flynn hunched against the statue and used it as protection against the shrieking wind.

When Shadows Creep

I could take refuge, up there, in the Manor. It's my right. All versions are under our protection, why can't I seek help from this one?

Flynn nodded to himself, agreeing with his thoughts. He left the bare spot blown clean by the gale and plunged into the snow. If he wandered too far from the path, drifts so tall that they cleared his shoulders threatened to overtake him. He would gain traction, though, and push through.

A light flickered in one of the windows, appearing like a golden guide. He'd never make it, he thought. But he aimed for that ember glow in the night, his only hope for warmth and direction in a version of this world he didn't belong in.

. . .

The Dark

It curled around the joist, giddy with the thought of Flynn being on the same plane, now. Where the Dark was strongest.

It glided along the wall until it pooled, smooth along the ground. It disappeared through a crack in the floorboards and spiraled along a railing until it reached the hard floorboards at the bottom.

It had been strange people that built this Manor; too tall, too broad to be normal humans. Humans, who in this land were part beast, and thus covered head to toe in thick, garish orange fur.

But those people were long gone. This place was long abandoned. They'd been driven away, farther into the mountains, far from where the Dark wanted to follow.

The Dark settled to the floor. It willed a fireplace into existence, then sparked a light that grew into a furious blaze.

Flynn would be too cold to be useful without it.

The temperature of the large empty room rose and the Dark shifted uncomfortably. It was necessary, and It shook back the discomfort.

It could see from the window, pressed against the glass, Flynn was struggling through the snow and the wind. His white-topped head disappeared in gusts and glittering ice.

Soon he'd be there.

And soon he'd see what the Dark truly was, and he would help It.

Flynn believed in this world, in this level of the undercurrent. He'd help the Dark escape It's confines.

It would climb inside of Flynn, inside his head, inside the very core of who he was in the undercurrent.

It would wrap around his skeleton and deep within his bones and Flynn, the key to travel through the multiverse, as a Guardian, as a Freemont, whatever that set him aside as part of the Dark, would open all the doors.

Infinite doors. Infinite worlds.

The Dark quivered with the thought.

Many of me, so many, It would be invincible.

When Shadows Creep

But now it should prepare. It couldn't be this version of itself, oh no. Not this scrambling and scurrying embodiment of shadows. It was a drift of wisp through this world, blacker than black, as it absorbed the light with no form of its own.

Oh no.

It caressed the glass and left a sooty mark streaked across Flynn on the other side, still struggling toward the light; a moth to the flame.

Something else. It had to be something else.

It pulled away from the window.

All those years it had existed in the shadows, in the corners of Freemont House. It had absorbed Flynn's thoughts and dreams, his aspirations, his desires for the Freemont House.

Flynn had been sent away, neglected, and abandoned by his fellows. They'd let him leave and left alone from their protective ranks.

The Dark had tried too hard, too quickly, to find a way into Flynn's mind at first. It had exposed him to too much of the bitter frostbitten cold that covered its soul and had damaged him. He'd awoken from a deep slumber, screams pouring from his lips. He screamed that he was blind, that he was damaged, and begged for the pain to stop.

He'd stumbled to the bathroom, tried to bathe away the sensation from his face and scalp. He had finally turned on the light. He'd fainted when he saw his new visage.

The Dark had retreated then. But it watched and waited. Flynn soon adapted.

And the Dark realized that Flynn could see it, now. Could see where it sat coiled amongst the rafters. He had encouraged it to come out, to make itself known. He spoke to the Dark long into the nights about his fears and hopes.

Flynn was so alone. And now he believed himself cursed. He believed the undercurrent had retaliated against his abandonment of the Manor and his encouragement of the Freemont House to blossom.

Flynn never discovered it was the Dark that cursed his eye. That killed his flesh; a perpetual frostbite that would never thaw.

And it was better that way. To be thrown out by Flynn, after all it had done to get into his good graces, would destroy it.

It would have returned to the sea and the dark and the deep. A fragment, a shred of its former self.

It would never have had this opportunity.

. . .

Caden

They marched along, a line of primary colors followed closely by a secondary. The sun blinded them and the air froze them. The driveway turned and twisted and rose so often that they frequently lost sight of Flynn. His sweater was a dark mark against the stone of the beasts that guarded the gate to the outside world, their only sightline. Caden feared they'd crest a hill and he'd disappear from them forever.

Caden wanted to break rank. He wanted to run. He wanted to go as quickly to Flynn's side as he could and absolve him of all wrongdoing. Flynn wasn't responsible for what he did, he must be under the control of whatever had shadowed the Manor. The dark lumps in his back were a disturbing sign of the creature that lurked beneath.

A creature that had tried to kill them all.

Caden had realized it all as he closed the door to the Manor behind him. That gesture had given him an extra bit of steel to wrap around his heart; protection for what needed to be done. He had almost died. He surely would have, along with Finnigan— obnoxious behavior and all— if the Manor hadn't slipped its manacles and thrown the staircase back into existence when it did.

It was lucky for Carmen that Roman had returned when he did, or Carmen too would have been dead, from exposure. The cold of the lair on the third floor would have destroyed, Carmen adrift in panic and lost to the elements.

Caden studied the back of Roman's head as they walked. He tried to place exactly where Roman said he had gone. Or *why* he had gone.

Who did he go see?

Caden's mind blurred. He tilted his head, urging the sensation to crawl out from under his skull.

Why can't I remember?

Caden scratched at his face and tucked his hands deeper into his pockets. His thumb caressed the trigger of the knife attached to his wrist, and he thought hard.

Carmen sent me to get Flynn. Carmen was instructed by Roman. Roman disappeared.

Something niggled at his brain and he frowned, biting his tongue, frustrated.

Carmen turned to look back at him and smiled, then pointed toward Flynn, "I don't think he's going anywhere, guys. I think he's made it into the undercurrent for once."

Finnigan muttered something about knobs or annoyances, and Roman nodded at Carmen's assessment.

"It'll be best if we pull him out of there, though, I can't imagine anything good coming from it," Roman said.

Caden nodded, half suspicious.

Something about Flynn being in the undercurrent alone made alarm bells pealed through his mind. What possible reason could there be for him to have gone there? Flynn did not walk between these worlds. It was a task left for Carmen and Roman alone. It was far too dangerous for the unskilled. They could become trapped. They could be killed on the far side and left a husk on this. Caden's mind reeled with the possibilities.

Chapter Twelve

Flynn

Flynn reached the door where a great steel handle jutted out from the aged and weathered wood. It was bitter cold in his grasp. He twisted as hard as he could and broke the crust of ice that had formed there. He threw his shoulder against the door hard, once, twice, as he attempted to break the seal of ice.

He cursed himself for being so small. The door was twice his height and twice the width of his wingspan. It denoted a people far larger than any normal humans -who already towered over Flynn- that once lived here.

But Flynn had an indomitable spirit on his side, as well as being completely numb from the cold. So, he fought with the door until it finally cracked open just enough to slip inside.

Flynn panted from the exertion and winced at the warmth that hit his bare skin the moment he stepped inside.

He marveled at the large empty room filled only with heat coming from the lone hearth that blazed away. Steam rose from his clothes and skin and the damp at his back sent chills down his spine.

He approached the fireplace with care, eyes always on the stairs that rose into the ceiling. Flynn stood as close as he could bear to the tongues of flames, his hands held out to the heat.

The light didn't quite reach into the hole in the ceiling. The dark of the second floor was as thick as tar. The fire's flicker cast his shadow across the floor, looming large in the dusty room. Lights and darks shifted, mesmerizing him.

Flynn thawed, every inch of his skin tingling as he warmed. The wind whistled between the bricks in the fireplace, flowed under the trim and the logs where the windows didn't quite fit; long fingers of cold that grasped at exposed flesh. Flynn stared at the top of the stairs, fear gripping at his neck and shoulders.

He had no idea what was going to come down those stairs.

He had no idea how to remove himself from the undercurrent.

What if I'm stuck here?

The sudden thought struck him as hard as a blow to the gut. He'd never been gone this long, this far. He'd never drifted beyond opening his eyes. The fire felt real enough, the cold, the drafts and the snow, all more than real. More than deadly.

This wasn't supposed to happen.

He didn't belong here. He should be as inconsequential as a shadow across this reality.

Flynn pinched his leg as hard as he could and muffled his squeal in response.

"Flynn," his name came as a whisper lifted high on a current, and drifted past his ear.

Flynn cringed. He curled back against the brick of the fireplace, hot against his spine.

The same humming tune that Flynn himself had played came lilting through the air. It was only slightly louder than the gale force winds outside. He had to strain to catch the eerie notes. He slid to the floor, wrapped his arms around his knees and tried to make himself small, unnoticeable, and irrelevant.

He didn't want to be there anymore.

Flynn squeezed his eyes shut, whispered under his breath, a plea to the undercurrent to let him leave, let him go, to return him to his world.

I promise I'll never come back.

He shoved his hands into the pouch of his pullover and squeezed the stone as hard as he could. Maybe it could hear him, the raven, and maybe it had the power to pull him home.

The humming stopped.

Flynn raised his eyes from his knees and gazed up at the top of the stairs. He could see something up there, something darker than the dark of the second floor, an outline of a figure, maybe. If he could trust his eyes not to play tricks on him. He took in a shudder of breath, closed both of his eyes, waited for a heartbeat, and then opened his disfigured one.

Like a light shone into the depths of a well, he could now see the figure clearly, outlined in a shimmer against the darkness of the upper room.

Someone was waiting for him.

Flynn gulped hard, his mouth suddenly dry. His stomach flipped. He attempted to speak but could only manage a croak. He cleared his throat and tried again, and he shouted up at the rafters, "I don't know who you are, but I only came here seeking shelter! I don't wish to bother you or this Manor, I'll be gone as soon as I can."

Silence.

"O-o-okay?" Less steady.

The figure moved as if to descend to where Flynn cowered, and then stepped away from the stairs, away from where Flynn could see.

Flynn opened both of his eyes and debated what to do. If he stayed down here, and it stayed up there, no one would be the wiser.

When Shadows Creep

No one would get hurt.

Footsteps thudded overhead, slow and heavy across the floor. Flynn froze to listen, breath held, and cocked his ear toward the ceiling.

The boom of the steps ceased somewhere above his head. The hair rose on the back of Flynn's neck and arms. He let out a small whimper.

No one would get hurt. No one would get hurt.

The fire flared outward and Flynn jumped back, pressing himself into the corner.

I don't want to be here anymore.

...

Finnigan

The Guardians had finally reached Flynn's small and frail form. His head rested against the stone of the beasts that guarded the Manor. They stared down at him with concern.

When Carmen and Roman slipped away, they were motionless, unconscious, and generally reduced to nothing more than a rigid sleeping form. Their passage to the under-current was noticeable for the way their eyes rolled back, whites of their eyes bright against long dark lashes.

Flynn however, was twitching. He reached out, grasping for what didn't exist, his head tossing back and forth in fear or anger or discomfort. He alternated between an eerie hum and a whisper in a language they couldn't quite discern. He kicked as if he tried to scramble backward against the stone.

Roman climbed the plinth and settled onto the stone. He pulled his scarf from around his neck to create a pillow for Flynn's tossing head. He held Flynn's face firmly with both hands, called his name, and stroked his face with his thumbs.

"Come out of it Flynn, come on, if you can hear me, follow my voice, can you hear me, Flynn? Come out of it, you don't belong there now, it isn't safe."

Flynn's eyelashes fluttered, one set tipped in gold at the end of their dark mahogany, the other snow white, the edges frosted in silver.

Carmen knelt and gripped Flynn's grasping hand, and held it tightly. "He's so cold."

Caden approached from the other side, rested a hand on Flynn's elbow. "You're right. How is he so cold? It isn't nearly cold enough out here for that, no matter how he's dressed. He's icy!"

Roman nodded in agreement and continued to study Flynn's face.

"It's the first you've seen him, isn't it?" Finnigan piped up, hands deep in the pockets of his coat, feet planted wide. He was staring pointedly at Roman.

When Shadows Creep

Roman tipped his head toward Finnigan in agreement but didn't look up.

"Looks a little different, huh, Roman?" Finnigan said.

Roman frowned, turned toward Finnigan, and sat back on his haunches. "What's your point, Finnigan? You seem to be nearing one, slowly."

Finnigan fished a hard candy from the depths of his pocket, crinkled the plastic, undressed the treat, and popped it into his mouth. The candy clicked against his teeth as he rolled it around. He folded the wrapper into a neat square, folded and folded until it would fold no more, and placed it back into his pocket.

He crossed his arms and stared down at Roman. "I think you already knew that this would happen, all of this. Some strange charade. For what end, I've no idea."

Roman raised one wild eyebrow, his eyes glinting in the bright sunshine, and he looked at Finnigan with a hardened stare. Finnigan braced himself, though whether for fight or flight, he couldn't quite tell.

"Guys, can we focus on Flynn, please? We'll resolve this when we're all together, here, okay? He's not safe in the undercurrent right now, not with that thing lurking under his skin," Caden said.

Caden was the first to move, he patted down the pockets of Flynn's pants. His fingers skimmed his socks and felt around his breast pocket. His hands finally landed on the hand that rested within the pouch of Flynn's sweater, and he pulled Flynn's arm free of the fabric.

His hand was clenched around a small round object, blacker than the darkest moonless night sky, his fingers tightened and stiff. Caden tried to pry it out of Flynn's hand. Flynn whimpered and pulled his arm tight across his body, cradling the stone against his chest.

"This has to be it," Caden said through gritted teeth. He tried once more to pull the object out of Flynn's grasp.

"You think the entity gifted this to him? During his dream? You think this is what he pulled back from the world it had sunk him into?" Roman inquired, his gazed focused on the darkness clutched in Flynn's hand.

Caden nodded and gave up, his large hands no match for the unexpectedly steely grip Flynn had on the stone. He sat down heavy on the plinth, head in his hands.

"You know you have to go in there, only blood can follow blood using the footsteps left across the under-current. You're the only one who can call him back from within,"

Carmen's voice was soft and hesitant, gaze steady on Finnigan. He had shuffled off, kicking at grass and rocks. He'd been ready for a fight and had been set aside for more important matters. Now, he stopped what he was doing, head still hung from his glare at the ground, and turned toward Carmen.

When Shadows Creep

"Me? No. I can't do that. I can't go in there, I don't know the first thing about finding anyone in there. You go," he said.

Carmen sighed, looked to Roman for help, but he wouldn't take his eyes away from the object in Flynn's hand.

"Finnigan, you and Flynn are brothers, whether you like it or not. The Freemonts. Every one of the Guardians, paired with another, so we have a connection to the home world from the undercurrent. No way for us to get lost. Always together, no matter what. You have to go. Neither Roman or I would be able to see him, he's not a part of us. Or we'd go in a second."

Finnigan cocked his head, spat the candy on the ground. "You maybe. Certainly not him," he raised his chin at Roman, who slowly raised his eyes to look back at him.

"Finnigan, whatever tantrum this is, whatever you'd like to accuse me of? It can wait. Please. Sit down here, take out your knife, and do what your brother needs you to do. Everything else can wait."

Roman rose from his position, hopped down from the platform from under the statue's wing, and gestured to the space he'd left behind. He waited for Finnigan to do exactly as he was told.

There was something of a shift happening here. Roman had left, and a hole had been created, one that initially was

Roman's shape and size, but had grown and stretched. It had been filled with misgivings and confusion.

And now Roman didn't quite fit back in from where he'd cut himself. And only Finnigan had the gumption to speak the worry aloud.

Flynn moaned, and it seemed to defrost Finnigan's frozen stance of defiance. He approached the statue, lifted himself up and sat cross-legged next to Flynn. He took the hand that held the stone, Flynn's fingers wrapped around it tightly, and rested it in his left palm.

Carmen nodded encouragingly, knife already at the ready, and with the tip, drew a small x onto the palm of his right hand. Caden used his own blade, dropped from his wrist, and marked the same onto the back of Flynn's hand.

"Remember, don't go in before the contact, blood of your blood isn't just a phrase. It's the key," Carmen warned.

Finnigan nodded and inhaled deeply, attempting to slow his heartbeat. Second nature to Carmen or Roman was still a shaky endeavor for Finnigan. He didn't want the audience, but was left without a choice. He placed his palm onto Flynn's hand, felt the small, short, spark that connected them, and exhaled slowly.

It was like tipping back too far in a chair. The one, heart-stopping moment of lift.

Except it doesn't stop. Didn't stop. For an eternity and a half, the only thing real and solid in the entirety of his proprioception was the cold of the egg and the heat of their blood.

Flynn.

The world ceased its spin. In a sudden snap his skeleton rocked with the recoil and he fell to his knees into cold, icy, snow.

. . .

Flynn

Flynn raised his head, the echo of Finnigan's voice in his brain and ears, and the sensation of warmth pooled on the back of his hand. He pulled the egg from his pocket, marveled at the coldness of it despite its proximity to his body.

He turned his hand over and saw the etched x in his flesh, already healed to a plain white scar, and stared down at it. Someone had needed his blood. Someone was trying to find him.

Finnigan.

He had two choices. He could take his chances out in blizzard, to be lost or frozen or swallowed up by the heaving drifts of snow, or he could climb the stairs. He could seek out whoever lurked in the floors above to find out why he was here and the significance of this place.

He would not solve anything by sitting, curled in on himself, waiting for something else to make his decisions

159

for him. Flynn rose shakily to his feet and pulled his sweater tighter around himself. In a world where he had no armor, no safety, no weapon, it was only his only protection against anything more than the elements.

He forced himself to take the first step, then another, foot after foot after foot, each one with the weight of his own insecurity dragging him to the floor.

The risers were an awkward height, far taller than his natural step, and he felt as if his knees ended up around his ears with every unsure stride he made. No banister here, no railing, nothing to cling to if he made a mistake. He reached a point two-thirds from the top when he realized that if whatever it was still lurked on this floor, it would see him rise above the floorboards far sooner than he would see it. And this left him open and vulnerable to all sorts of attacks.

But what could he do?

Flynn cautiously moved one more stair up, and a glint of metal caught his eye. It appeared that the people who had designed this Manor didn't have a complete disregard for safety. An ornate metal railing enclosed the three stair-less sides of the opening, and masked Flynn's head from view. He dropped to his knees and crawled the remainder of the stairs with his breath held.

It was a solid silence, full of unsaid words and thick with unmeasured potential. Like the calm of thunderstorms before the atmosphere collapsed.

When Shadows Creep

Flynn exhaled.

A thunder of footsteps overhead burst from one corner of the room and stampeded to the other. They faded as they ascended. Another staircase must be on this level, his now-quarry fled to the third floor.

Unless it was a trap. A lure, an excuse to pull him away from the door to outside.

The temperature dropped several degrees on this floor. There was no fire to warm the room and the ambient heat from the lower level only rose to take the edge off the air. Flynn cautiously rose to his feet, climbed the last stair, and crouched next to the railing. He used it as a shield from any potential third person, who may have remained silent and watchful while the other became a distraction.

Another wide, empty space where dust covered the floor. It seemed strange that not a single leaf or piece of debris of any sort littered the floor in any direction. Flynn began to think that not even mice dared enter this place. He could see the footprints in the dust from what must be the other entity in this place. They seemed to start at the stairs, crossed the room to where the chimney continued up to the floor above, and then dissolved into a path of smears towards the darkened staircase in the corner.

This building didn't make sense. It was more like a doll-house, something crudely designed and built by a child with only a rudimentary understanding of what a house was for, and what a house should look like. There were two windows on the front side, two windows on the backside. They were evenly spaced, equally sized. A wooden box, three stories high, sat with absolutely nothing inside.

Flynn's thoughts reeled. What world was this, that the Manor was such a sham of its other selves? Every single version of every single room Flynn had seen had been elegant, tailored rooms detailed and well-appointed. Even rooms that decided to be temporarily garish were still fully furnished.

Underneath the emptiness he could feel the heart of the Manor that thrummed away, though. When his hand brushed the floorboards, he could almost hear its hum, even through the soles of his socked feet. The beating core was still there, but so very weak.

It crippled his own heart to feel the absence of that vibrancy.

He absently kissed his fingertips, pressed them to the floor. No matter how far from *his* world, and *his* Manor, he wanted it to know he was there. He hoped that it heard him. Maybe it'd be the thing that would save him from this place.

The footsteps rang out over his head, a light patter, rain-like. A flicker in the corner of his eye, and he abruptly turned his head toward the movement.

Nothing was there. The waft of a breeze moved across his skin, a breath, maybe, on the back of his neck.

When Shadows Creep

Flynn spun, ready to lunge, his hands splayed. But nothing but dark and dust stared back.

Flynn worked his way along the wall, hand to the boards, felt that thump, thump through his palm.

It's your own pulse, idiot. This Manor can't help you.

The thought slid its way across his brain, and he shook his head and continued along his path, silent. He had reached the bottom of the stairs, the last staircase he hoped. His nerves couldn't take any more floors. Flynn felt suffocated like he would drown in this dark and this quiet.

Flynn.

It was Finnigan's voice again, somewhere at the back of his brainstem. The mark on his hand throbbed. He clutched it in his other, held it close to his chest. Something had happened to his body, back outside of the undercurrent, he was sure of it. The ghostly sensation of fingertips on his wrists and the back of his neck crawled across his skin. They flitted across his temples. He struggled against the panic it drew out of him, from deep down in his stomach.

It was like being covered in bugs or worms or crawling things that wanted beneath the cuffs of his sleeves and into his socks. He wanted to scream.

Flynn.

This time, Roman's voice. Flynn stopped his squirming and cocked his head, listened again for his name to be called.

The sensation ceased, but he continued to twitch, unable to shrug away the memory.

He moved toward the stairs, determined to confront whatever lay ahead of him.

...

Caden

Caden stood to the side, hands jammed into the pockets of his jacket.

Carmen sat, legs crossed, wrists rested on knees, palms up, and stared down at the unconscious brothers. Finnigan had slipped away far quicker than expected. It was possible he'd been practicing, but it may have been the urgency of the situation and the blood connection that had helped him along. It would have pushed him through the door with no more than a concerned glance.

Roman knelt by Flynn's head and repeatedly tried to connect. He tried to call him back and was having no luck, his hands pressed to Flynn's temples, his lips almost on Flynn's forehead as he called.

Caden's foot tapped away on the wet ground. The damp in the air clung to his hair, slicked his skin. He wiped at his brow and wished for a hot shower.

They should've just left Flynn alone. He was fine, Caden thought. *He was fine without us.*

Something hitched in his chest at the thought, and he rubbed absently at the spot over his heart.

Caden glanced upward, a quick uptick of his eyes, and caught Carmen's gaze. Something passed between them, a flicker of understanding. He followed Carmen's eyes as they shifted to Roman, and then back to Caden. Caden shrugged in response, mouthed the question on his lips.

Carmen's eyes bored into him.

"Hey Roman, why don't you give it a rest? Let Finnigan find him. He's got this, just let him pull Flynn back. He's obviously not responding to you." Caden approached as he spoke, and reached for Roman's shoulder.

Roman turned. His glare burned into Caden and stopped him dead in his tracks. He wavered, unsure whether to proceed or to remain in his place.

Roman closed his eyes, considered for a moment, and then shifted to sitting. He groaned as he took the pressure off of his knees and rested his back against the statue. He stared up at the statue, at the great claws that curled over his head and sighed. "It's all my fault,"

Caden and Carmen gaped, not believing that he admitted a wrongdoing to one of their own.

"I told him to go. I told him there was something out there for him. I told him that he didn't have to stay, that he could create his own House. There was something special about that boy, I knew it since the day he walked through the doors of the Manor and I've known it every moment since."

Roman swallowed hard and looked down at Flynn's prone face. His fingertips crawled along the stone of the statue and stroked Flynn's hair, the whiteness of the damaged strands bright against his dark skin.

"This poor boy. I thought he'd be safe. He's so…," Roman inhaled deeply. "He's so *inconsequential*. I didn't think he'd be a target. I was so, so wrong. And then it found him. I knew it had, and yet I waited. I wanted to see what it wanted. And then it touched him. It touched him and changed him, preyed on his insecurities. And I knew I'd made a horrible mistake,"

Roman put his face in his hands and began to weep silently.

The words had poured out of him so swiftly, so violently. Their sudden stop seemed violent, too. A small sound escaped Roman, from between his fingers. It was a cross between an inhale and a sob. But when his eyes peered over his fingertips, they were dry, his gaze steely as he stared off across the farm fields.

His hands dropped to his knees. "And then, I thought, safety in numbers. We'll have Flynn back, he'll be safe. We'll keep him safe. I, I could keep him safe."

Carmen reached across Flynn and Finnigan and offered a hand to Roman. He reached for it, and briefly touched fingertips to palm. Then he lowered his hand, as if he were unworthy of the comfort.

"And now we're all in terrible danger," he said.

Caden faltered a half step forward and shifted uneasily. "Roman, from what? What could possibly hurt all of us, if we stick together to fight it?"

Roman touched Finnigan's hand on top of Flynn's, where the stone lay between their palms.

"This is proof that the Darkness that touched Flynn, and wrapped itself around his heart, can move between the shifts. Flynn brought this back with him from somewhere the Dark built, a shoddy reality that fooled him into thinking he was awake.

"This dark fills the world with evil things that lurk in the night and the cold. It gave him this stone to prove that it can slip through the cracks in the worlds. The Manor is a wide open door to all of every reality, of every eternity, so long as it can get inside one of us to let it through." He pulled his hand back from Finnigan's and twisted it in his other. He ran his thumb over and over the back of his hand as if he tried to rub away a mark only he himself could see.

Caden made an abortive move toward Roman, whether to fight him or to reassure him, he wasn't certain. But Roman continued anyway.

"And it's chosen Flynn, it's built a relationship with him. A tenuous connection, an understanding, and it used that, that stone, as a conduit to pull them together," he said.

167

Caden looked down at the entwined hands of Flynn and Finnigan. "So how do we take it away from him? You tried to pry it out of his fingers, he wouldn't let it go."

Roman shook his head. "I haven't a clue. I've never seen anything like this happen before. My best and only guess would be that he has to let it go in the undercurrent, or destroy it if it's possible, and then it will fall from his grasp in this world. It might even simply fade away. We'd have to be wary of it. Take it from him, find a way to destroy it. He may be irrationally attached to it, may even be paranoid that we'd steal it. I think that's what lead him out here. To get the stone as far away from us as possible, while still being close to the Manor."

"Well, it would've been helpful to let Finnigan know that before he left," Carmen groaned.

Roman's shoulders sagged, deflated and withdrawn. His eyes were unfocused as he stared down at his feet.

"How'd we get so attached to these little guys in so little time?" Carmen's mouth twisted wistfully with the question.

"Little time being comparative," Caden smirked.

"Over seventy-five years is just a drop in a bucket, huh?" Carmen smiled.

Caden's cold hands were jammed once more in his pockets. He tried so very hard not to shiver and shudder as he smiled at Carmen. Where once it had been only Flynn's skin that had been freezing cold, it seemed now that the very air that surrounded him was affected. Infected even, by rolling cold that poured around him. If he squinted at Finnigan and Flynn, he could almost see that their lips were tinged with blue. But maybe it was a trick of the light.

Roman's arms were wrapped around himself. Carmen was in a similar stance. Caden assumed they felt it just as much, if not worse, than he did. It wouldn't be long before the cold would be utterly unbearable.

Caden stomped his feet, paced in a circle, and realized the farther away he was, the warmer the air was. He reveled in the kiss of the sun on his skin, and the way his hands thawed in the warmth.

Caden turned and called back to the others. "Alright, so next step then, say we do see Flynn drop the stone thing. If he drops it? How do we destroy it? What will destroy it? What is it even made of?"

Carmen leaned forward over Finnigan and gestured, hand out to Roman. "Do you have your pocket watch? The one with the diamonds along the clasp?"

Roman cocked an eyebrow and pulled it from deep within the inner breast pocket of his jacket. He zipped the jacket back up as quickly as he'd unzipped it. He withdrew into the high neck, his face buried to warm his chin and nose.

Carmen gripped the watch like a skipping stone and rubbed the object in Flynn's hand with the edge of the diamonds. A horrible, high pitched singing sound emitted when it made contact, as Carmen tried to scratch at the stone, tried to discern what it was made of. Despite the angry sound it issued, and how hard Carmen scratched until Caden's ears felt like they bled from the noise, the egg remained unmarred. It was completely free from the abuse of the diamonds.

Carmen sat back, head tilted, and studied the egg.

"Here Caden, feel this. The diamonds have warmed from the friction and the contact,"

"I'll take your word for it, Carm," Caden kept his hands firmly in his pockets. When Carmen returned it to Roman, he inspected it carefully, rubbed at the worn bronze with his thumb. "Strange," he said.

He held up his hand and showed the others the sooty streak across his thumb. The more he wiped at his hand, the farther the mess smeared across his skin.

Roman stared down at his hand as the darkness spread across his palm, darker than charcoal, darker than the night.

"Oh it's burning, oh, oh no," Roman clutched at one hand with the other, the black spreading as frost crawled across his palm.

He half-fell from his seat on the statue to the ground, and furiously wiped his hand on the grass, trying to remove the blackness from his palm.

Caden and Carmen looked on worriedly, and joined him on their knees in the grass. Caden offered his handkerchief.

When Shadows Creep

The grass where Roman wiped began to wilt and brown, growing darker and darker. It rotted away until it was nothing more than sludge, like what you might find at the bottom of a bucket left to rot in the sun. Each blade of grass that blackened touched the next, and it grew, an ever-growing circle of death, expanding ever outward.

The Guardians scrambled backward on hands and feet as fast as they could. The radius of dying vegetation petered out after a broad circle, maybe eight feet across, the edges merely sad and wilted.

Roman lay still and panted in the grass, his eye level with the destruction to the turf.

"One drop. One drop of darkness did this much damage. This much cold… it will kill everything. Flynn— no one, the worlds— they will not survive if this grows and replicates throughout eternity. It'll all be a wasteland."

Caden flopped backward and stared up at the blue of the cloudless sky. Heretofore he'd never imagined scenarios of death and the destruction of everything they strove to protect. Now, those scenarios ran through his head.

Poor Flynn. No wonder he was damaged…

"When you said it touched him, you really meant it. What happened to his face, oh my God," Carmen's head dropped as the others looked at the patch of death where grass once grew.

Chapter Thirteen

Flynn

Flynn retreated to the first floor and jabbed his pocket knife into a crack in the thick wooden mantel. The sweat beaded on his brow as he tried to lever a piece of the thick timber away from the rest. He had decided he couldn't continue in the dark without a light. He would not go up to the third floor half blind and uncertain of what waited for him.

He would make a torch if it killed him.

He'd freed about a third of the length and put his full weight behind the lever. The crack echoed in the silent Manor. He hoped that it could be mistaken for the crackle of the fire, the pop of the logs. He hoped that the entity did not come down the stairs to investigate why he'd fled.

The knife was buried to the hilt and he hung his full weight on the knife, pulling his feet up off the floor. He hung for a split second before the rest of the wood came splintering off the mantel. He tumbled to his knees and held aloft his prize.

When Shadows Creep

He was left with a three-foot splinter of a dark, ancient wood. Flynn tore at the bottom of his sweater, ripped a strip he could wrap around the end, and tied it off tightly. There was no real fuel to soak the fabric in, so once it caught fire, he'd have to move fast, up and up. He'd have to run up those too-high stairs and hope it remained lit long enough to give him a good view of his foe.

But it was the only hope he had.

The tendrils of cold in the air touched the exposed skin at his back and waist. He waited to hear if any sound reached him, any clue that the intruder had moved. No sound came back to him, no echo or patter or word from above. So, he plunged his handmade torch into the flame and waited for the sweater to catch, brilliant and bright, and held it out in front of him. He took a deep breath, and straightened the edge of his shirt.

Now or never.

He charged toward the stairs.

By the time he reached the second floor his knees were screaming at him. He stopped, reeling with the burning pain. The second floor remained as empty as it had before. If anything, the air had chilled further. In the light of the flame he saw his breath, could see how blue his fingers had become. And again, he charged toward the stairs and toward the unknown.

...

Finnigan

Finnigan struggled through the snow, the drifts far higher than his waist. His only guide in the dark was the far-off flicker of firelight and the dark hulking shape of a building black against the black sky. He squinted as ice whipped about his face and coated his eyelashes. The slush froze to his cheeks, clung to his skin, and frosted his hair.

He hoped against hope that Flynn had made it to the Manor. He prayed that Flynn wasn't buried somewhere in these shifting dunes of frigid snow. He would never find him if he were.

But the pulse in his hand, the warm spot on his palm that throbbed with the magic of their shared blood, told him another story. He was alive. And if he was anything like Finnigan, then he was out there.

Exactly like me, let's be honest, he thought.

So he chose to believe that Flynn was there, waiting out this unwelcome trip into the undercurrent. He'd be inside and safe from this strange world, between walls that featured a version of the Manor Finnigan had never ever seen. This was a world of ice. There was nothing more, nothing beyond, nothing ahead. If this Manor shifted, it was into one more frozen prison after another.

When Shadows Creep

Finnigan's hands were shoved into his armpits to combat against the cold. He'd left behind their world prepared for a Massachusetts fall. For a crispness in the air, maybe, in his brilliant colored jacket. But it was light and unlined. Waterproof, for certain, but no better than paper against this gale-force wind.

He rocked head down, hood up, and took another forceful step forward. The trail behind his feet was washed away over and over by the screaming storm. He swore the Manor was no closer, no matter how hard he strained Oh, how his thighs and calves ached. He understood, now, why Flynn had been so cold on his spot on the statue. The effect of the undercurrent was strong enough, the magic powerful in this unwanted space, to affect his body back in his own reality.

The thought terrified Finnigan.

If the Darkness had constructed this with the energy of the undercurrent, then the entity was far more powerful than they had ever suspected.

Finnigan pushed forward for another step, and his toe caught a rock or a branch, something hidden beneath the snow. He fell into a soft hillock of snow. It felt as though he fell forever, the whiteness all around him, blinding and suffocating. He clawed his way back out, gasping for air, and fumbled for what he'd tripped on. It could maybe be used as a weapon, whatever it was.

The thing was buried so deep that as he tugged, he nearly lost his balance and fall backward into the drift behind him. But it came free, and he held it up.

It was an arm bone, likely a humerus, far longer and larger than any human arm he'd ever seen. Tattered clothing, dark in color, indiscernible in the half light, still clung to it, wrapped tightly around the bone.

Finnigan shuddered but hefted it in his hand. The weight was an unexpected comfort, and he was glad that his damaged shoulder wasn't on his proficient side.

Better than nothing.

He pushed off once more, struggling for traction where his loafers slipped on the packed down snow. Slowly he gained momentum. His pants were soaked through, and clung to his legs in cold and limp twists, no longer useful against the harsh cold. A stream of swear words flung away in the blackness around him, useless against the cold, just like his pants.

Finnigan raised his head and realized he'd made some progress. The Manor seemed to have hopscotched toward him, impossibly, and he wondered if the Darkness had made a misstep. A glitch in this corner of the undercurrent was a mistake that he could use as a shortcut. It served to increase his determination, and he picked up speed.

He soon crashed against the heavy wooden door, the slick boards under his hands, and he breathed hard. Finnigan lowered his hood, and pulled hard on the handle, and found that it hadn't quite closed behind whoever entered last. Flynn had to be here. No sane resident of this darkened place would have left the door ajar. It was suicide.

The door was perfectly silent and glided smoothly across the powdery fine snow that drifted and blew around the entrance. He slipped carefully between the door and the jamb, his bone club lifted and at the ready for anyone who lurked in the shadows.

The fire roared off to his right and the heat from the blaze seared the tip of his nose and cheekbones. The soft points of the tips of his ears burned. The feeling in his fingers was already returning, and his pants and coat dripped slush with every step toward the fireplace. He ran his hand along the mantle, a gash stretched across the soot-darkened wood, lighter than the rest and freshly exposed.

He could still feel a residual tingle from Flynn's touch that had seeped into the woodgrain. He was alive, and he had been there.

The undercurrent recognized when something didn't belong. Guardians left trails in the undercurrent. Minute smears of energy that should exist on another plane but marked the one in which they currently resided.

If he squinted, he could see a footprint trail of them that lead first toward the stairs, and then back again.

He had forgotten Flynn had been in socks. The thought gave him pause, the wild outdoors still too fresh in his mind, the struggle it had been to get to this Manor.

"That idiot is going to lose a foot," Finnigan muttered under his breath. He cocked his head to listen to any sound coming from the overhead floors. He debated removing his own shoes, to give himself the benefit of a soundless approach. But a quick escape out into the night, if they were pursued, would leave him no better than Flynn.

They'd fall out of the undercurrent while in this Manor, or not at all.

Finnigan was once more hyper-aware of just how vulnerable they were outside of their own reality. Their immortality in their own reality, their exaggerated resistance to injury, and their immunity to illnesses were important for their safety around the liminal spaces. It made sure they could protect what they'd sworn never to abandon.

But once they pushed through, they were no different than regular humans or creatures that live in the alternate spaces. The thought sent a piercing blade of panic through Finnigan's chest.

"Finnigan."

Carmen's voice was soft and clear in his ear, though he remained alone in the fire lit room. He was being called, through the undercurrent, from their reality. But he couldn't leave, not yet. He hadn't found Flynn. Flynn was all that mattered, and he certainly wasn't going to slip back and forth with any great ease. He wasn't Carmen.

Finnigan waited for another message, an indication that he should stop or wait for further instructions. But none came.

Then came the ghostly sensation of fingers on his wrist, then pressure, as if someone was encircling it and squeezing. He held his hand aloft and the scar on his palm glowed faintly in the half-light. He felt a tap on the back of his hand, one, then two more after a brief pause.

Finnigan took a deep breath, held it, cleared his head, and tried to listen to the background hum of the cosmos. Tried to listen far beyond the wild roar of the wind outside and the crackle of the fire. Past the white noise in his head. Communication was so forced, so brief, in the undercurrent. Mere ripples in the pond of time, as they breached through layer after layer of versions of the world.

"Get...stone...stone...Flynn...Finnigan."

The voice was no more a whimper echoing from the opposite end of an empty room. It was Carmen's voice but it was distorted by time and space.

Finnigan stood so still that his pulse drummed a steady beat in his ears, a rising thud as his heartbeat quickened.

Of course he had to get the stone from Flynn. He hadn't seen much of it, but he knew it was likely the source of his trance-like state. It was an uneasy connection between this shadowy corner of existence and where their bodies remained. The Flynn in *this* world might have other ideas about what to do with the stone.

Finnigan hoped this would be a rescue mission with a victim willing to be saved.

If Flynn had dug in, had been convinced that he belonged here, that his consciousness deserved this Purgatory-like existence, there wasn't much Finnigan could do to bring him back. He would have to leave him here. And he would die.

Finnigan was in no way prepared for this.

Just days ago, Finnigan had spent his days in leisure as he read, wrote, and slammed the front door in the face of any human who managed to get far enough up the driveway to use the heavy bronze knocker. And now he was here, wielding a bone for a weapon, frozen deep beneath his skin, hair slick to his scalp, and wondering if he could save his brother.

. . .

Flynn

Tiny pieces of flaming sweater fluttered around Flynn's face and hands like drunken deranged butterflies. They caught on the drafts and whispered about his face.

When Shadows Creep

He stood at the top of the stairs, the very top, where the great gabled roof stretched over his head. It reached far beyond where the light touched, boasting massive timbers that belied how solid this building was. About half of his torch still remained. It had lasted much longer than he had guessed when he had lit it, and he was thankful for it.

The cloaked figure sat perfectly still in the center of the massive room, their hood raised and shrouded in dark. No glint of light reflected from eyes or skin, like a black hole. A black hole as destructive as any that existed in the depths of the universe, and it was staring back at him. The air had become so cold that it sucked the pressure from the room. The atmosphere was so thin that Flynn almost felt like he was drowning.

He tried to control his lungs, tried to prevent himself from taking short gasps that would surely make him pass out.

Deep in through his nose, slow out through his mouth.

He stood perfectly motionless. The entity towered over him, hands (if it had hands) must have been clasped together in front of it, its arms covered by the long sleeves of its robe.

It waited.

Flynn waited.

He couldn't move his arms, his legs, his feet. He was close to being unable to breathe. Flynn was afraid to confront

what had haunted his sleep, the moments between uncon-
sciousness and wakefulness, the being that had haunted the
edges of every moment he lived. The thing that had created
spaces that should not exist and had slipped through every
minute fracture in his mind that it could find.

Why did it wait?

Flynn imagined it was searching for the best way to tear
him limb from limb. That it was imagining which bone to
crack first. Pulling, pulling at his skin. Nibbling, tearing, and
neatly dismembering him as easily as a roast chicken. Or,
maybe it would absorb his soul; pull it angrily from Flynn's
body. A moment of violence, a swirl of dark and depth
before his mind collapsed in on itself.

Every possible scenario the very worst that could
happen. The most violent, the most bloody he could imagine, these were the images that flitted in and out of his brain,
uncontrollable and unwanted. Flynn began to shake. from
nerves, from fear, the cold, from unanswered adrenaline.

And still, It stood. It watched him.

Flynn started to consider that it wasn't really a person.
Maybe a coat had been left to dry on a coat rack...

...In the middle of the room, on the top floor of an
abandoned house.

Yes obviously, that's exactly it, Flynn thought, and he
almost rolled his eyes at himself.

When Shadows Creep

An ember drifted down from the torch and landed on the back of his hand. He winced but resisted the urge to brush it from his skin. He watched it sizzle and evaporate, leaving a tiny stream of smoke in its wake. He blew on the hot spot, ever so slightly, and he focused on the pain. It steadied him.

"Hello, Flynn." The voice was syrupy, sickly sweet but deep. It rolled with oiled edges and the words rounded with smoke and fire. The pitch of the voice left Flynn feeling hollow, as if something so much larger and darker and older than himself had opened its eyes and seen that he existed for the very first time.

And it was not pleased by that fact.

"What are you?" He asked, swallowing back the shake in his voice. He flushed. He couldn't sound so weak in the face of something that considered him so insignificant.

The hood stared at him and slowly shifted. It tilted to the side as if it was considering him, looking deep within his body and finding his blood, his bones, and his soul. It looked at him as if it could reach inside and pluck his heart from beneath his ribs and hand it to him.

Flynn couldn't see a face, no distinguishing features, but he didn't need to. He perceived its stare. Its gaze was directed at him, and him alone. It could spend an eternity with Flynn in its scrutiny, and it would know every inch of every possible version of himself he could ever be.

That voice rang out once more, a subtle reverberation in the floor boards as it spoke. "Do you enjoy this place? This level of your worlds, lost and forgotten? Discarded at the very bottom of the heap of abandoned domains, vanished realities, unworthy of the Guardians?"

The words quickly gilded themselves in venom and dripped with disdain and sarcasm.

Flynn shuffled through his thoughts and memories. He tried to remember anything Roman or Carmen may have said about worlds such as this. Worlds that were no longer accessed through the liminal spaces, abandoned by the undercurrent.

He could think of nothing, no time when that had ever been the case.

The Manor cherished the worlds in which it existed. It reveled in the tiny details, pulling pieces from dark places and light spaces. It pushed them together and lovingly mended them to the corners of its own self. It kept them until it needed to shift and change, and then it carefully stored them away in the undercurrent.

Flynn couldn't imagine the Manor would have discarded any piece of the multiverse, no matter how dismal or destructive.

It just wasn't how things worked.

"We'd never— We've never— You're wrong," Flynn sputtered.

When Shadows Creep

The torch flickered and the flame faded to nothing more than a red glow close to Flynn's face. Just as Flynn dreaded it would extinguish and leave him in the dark with this creature, it found another bit of life and flared up, brightening once more.

Flynn realized the cloaked figure had used this temporary distraction and moved closer, ever silent. Flynn tried to still the tremble that had found its way into his fingertips. No breath or sound came from it or its movement. The only indication was the air, far more icy now that it was nearer.

"Am I? Am I truly, Flynn? They abandoned you. You're one of them, you should mean more to them than anything. And yet you were discarded the moment you believed in yourself. Left to die. What is a world such as this to them, if they couldn't even keep you?"

A shadow crept across the back of his brain. *They never came for me. Not until it was too late.*

He pushed away the thought, squeezing the egg in his pocket a little harder. Even still, he could feel the doubt, tentative fingers at the base of his skull as they tried to pry into his mind.

"Do you really think they brought you back because they missed you? Because they *needed* you? No." The Darkness moved forward another step, bent from its height to lower its visage closer to Flynn.

Flynn stared deep into the depths of the hood and still could not see a sign of anything within. Now, when it spoke, he could feel the vibration in his chest and his ribs, could feel it rumble down his spine.

"No, Flynn. They brought you back to the Manor so they could prove you hadn't *ruined them*. Destroyed their way of life. They brought you back to stifle the flame that you sparked under your own hands, your own fingertips. A destruction so vast and natural that it would blossom into a new way of life and living."

Flynn tried to step away and faltered, his foot rocking on the edge of the stairwell. The hand that carried the torch wind-milled to keep his balance, and the torch swung toward the cloaked figure.

It hissed and stepped back, its head swaying side to side, slow and measured. Flynn clutched the torch in both hands to keep it between himself and the *thing*.

"Th-they worried about me! They were worried about what happened to me alone in the Freemont House. They brought me home to take care of me!"

Its laugh filled the chambers to the rafters with an indescribable heaviness, a treacle-rich sound, velvety-smooth. It echoed through the empty room.

The pressure in the room increased. The wind outside that once howled as it streamed around the rooftop, silenced. Flynn took a deep breath. A scream was trying to claw its way up his throat, unwanted and unneeded.

Just like me.

He shook his head but his skin began to crawl, his neck flushed. He couldn't help but believe that maybe he'd been wrong. Maybe this darkness knew the truth better than he. Maybe it could see what was in him, in all of them, and maybe it was right.

"You're powerful Flynn, all alone in your own right. You created a House with no one's help, no one's instruction. You did what was natural to you. You crossed between worlds and into the undercurrent and you fed those flames. No one else could have done that.

"You and I, we're the same. Creators. *Changers.* We make the worlds more than they could ever be on their own. Don't you want to feed that? Nurture it into something more beautiful?"

A hand extended toward him, the sleeve slipped back. Its skin was so very white, but the nails were a ferocious scarlet. In its outstretched hand sat an egg just like the one he possessed.

"We need you, Flynn. More than them, more than anything. Together, we can create something wonderfully evil and powerful. I know how you're drawn to the seed. To the beauty of it, to its darkness, cold and deep. It speaks to something within you. You have no idea how to harness it.

K. Brooks

I can help you and we'll be greater than anything the multiverse has ever seen."

The egg— *seed*— seemed to grow in its hand, turning and rolling glossy and dark. The firelight absorbed by its obsidian midnight. It called to the one in his pocket, alluring and smoky, like the smell of bonfires on a summer night mixed with dewy grass and wet earth. It spoke of crystalline Christmas nights and the world on the edge of the New Year. That moment of change, of promise, of perspective, when the world holds its breath and waits.

Flynn was taken back to those nights on the playground. Those nights when the leaves were strewn across the ground laced with frost; when the stars twinkled overhead, far closer to Earth than any other time of year; the nights when it felt as if the world pulled the Milky Way in and absorbed the cold beyond the moon.

Oh, and the moon. It rode high, a white lady in an elegant dance with the forces of nature. The clouds always ragged ribbons as they drifted quickly across her, an illusion, torn to tatters in the night.

That was when Flynn felt most alive.

And here was the opportunity to make the *whole world* as beautiful as those autumn nights. Here was his opportunity to make everything as crisp and fresh and new as that first blast of icy air.

When Shadows Creep

Flynn took a deep breath and pulled his own stone from his pocket. He cradled it against his chest. It seemed to hum, and it too began its slow revolution, same as the other. He gazed down at it and wondered at its beauty. He couldn't see the Darkness smile, couldn't see any face at all, but he could *feel* it. He could feel the beam of it, the stretch of the muscles around a mouth that didn't exist, under eyes that couldn't see.

It was the smile of the damned.

The thought flickered and caught flame.

The scent, once so pleasant, a reminder of dreams and of times spent wasted away in awe of the stars, now reminded him of the grave. The cold hard earth, of dead things and bitter winds; a never-ending winter. The sky blackened and the ground turned to ash. The sunshine and the green things were no more.

This is what the Darkness truly promised, behind its infatuation with the beauty of the night. And it would destroy the multiverse. Every reality smothered in darkness, shriveled into twisted and dead shadows of themselves. It would spread, a plague to the realities, and it would use the thinness of reality, the liminal spaces, to break its way through and corrupt it all. Everything.

Flynn closed his hand around the stone. "No."

The Darkness pulled back the hand that held the stone and it disappeared once more into the fold of heavy fabric. A rattlesnake warning rose in the air around them, the very wood of the building shook in response to Flynn's declaration.

"They won't want you back. *You're tainted*, never to be whole again. You could never be a real Guardian again. You can't go back, Flynn, not from this."

Flynn gulped and took a step back.

He needed to leave. He'd take his chance with the snow. Flynn would find his way out of the undercurrent and return to the others.

He took another half-step, teetering on the edge of the staircase. The Darkness ceased its rattle, a deep and uneasy breathing coming from the hood as if it struggled not to become enraged.

"How dare you!"

The winds picked up outside and the rafters moaned as the crawl of the air teased at the decrepit shingles and tried to fight their way in. It felt as if the sky were trying to peel away the rooftop, or like it was trying to reach in and remove him, fling him away into the ebony of the ever-night where he'd be lost forever.

The torch had burned down to a dying glow, the end of the baton red-hot mere inches from the top of his fist.

The Darkness lunged.

Flynn tripped backward and began to fall.

When Shadows Creep

...

Finnigan

Finnigan heard the entire conversation from where he hovered in the stairwell. He had heard the warning rattle of whatever entity Flynn spoke to. He had heard the wind as it crashed against the Manor like waves on a cliff, the ferocity of the storm all-consuming.

He could feel the outer walls of the stone being scoured by the snow and the ice as they eroded away into oblivion.

He didn't want to be here when the storm broke through.

And then Flynn had taken a stand. He'd denied the entity what it looked for so deep within him.

Finnigan could see Flynn's socked feet. He could see his red flesh where it poked through a hole in the heel. Whatever he spoke to was beyond his sight line and he wavered, unsure of what to do.

When it spoke of the Guardians' abandonment, of them no longer needing Flynn, a kernel of guilt began to grow in his heart. He'd done terrible things in his lifetime to prevent the humans from trespassing. He'd done all he could when patches in reality became too unstable for humans. He'd fought them— he'd even killed once or twice. But they'd been accidents. They'd rested heavy on his heart.

There were nights when he awoke feeling as if everything would collapse in around him and dissolve his existence from that plane. But it was for the greater good, or so he kept telling himself.

There was nothing Flynn had done, or would do, that could ever make him or the other Guardians abandon him. Not truly. He realized it now. He'd told Flynn he was dead to him, but that was never true. Not really.

When he left, Flynn took up residence in a corner of Finnigan's mind; a constant reminder that Finnigan's last words to his brother had been out of anger. He'd never forgive himself if something happened to that boy, something that could have been avoided.

Finnigan had ruminated in these thoughts, but then Flynn suddenly took a step back. The world seemed to slow around Finnigan. He reached for Flynn, cradling his falling shoulders. As frail as he'd become, he still knocked Finnigan back into the wall. Finnigan crumpled to his knees and slid down the stairs.

But Flynn was fine. Flynn was here, and Finnigan had caught him. Flynn and Finnigan stared for a moment into each other's faces, Flynn's eyes full of confusion and hurt. But then the Dark swooped down as it screeched and clawed toward them.

They fell the few remaining steps and slid side by side, Flynn's hand still wrapped around the dying torch. They flipped to their backs in unison, tried to scramble to their feet. Flynn was successful and staggered away to the center of the room, but Finnigan was pinned and the Darkness scratched at his face and arms.

· · ·

Flynn

Flynn stumbled forward and lined up the swing with his glowing staff. It had reduced to a brilliant glowing ember. He swung a heavy blow into the middle of the heaving black shadow and it shrieked, exploding into hundreds of ragged streamers of darkness. They fluttered around them, Finnigan on the ground curled over his knees, his hands raised over his face in protection.

Flynn reached for Finnigan and hauled him up, unsteady on his feet. They leaned against each other, both uneasy, both unsteady, and nervous laughter bubbled up from deep within them. They turned toward the adjoining staircase and were stopped dead.

The shadow had reassembled, a great hulk of a shape, and it hissed. No longer cloaked, now merely formless. Waves of cosmic cold washed over them, rippling through the air in a thick wave.

Flynn drowned in the darkness of the ocean. He could almost taste the salt and the sand, could almost feel the tickle at the back of his throat.

"I will not be denied the multiverse. I will spread. And you will help me if it's the last thing you do."

Flynn began to sink down, down. It was too cold, too dark. He would soon reach the bottom of the great black sea. The waves crashed overhead. He would touch the bottom where no light would ever reach. He released the torch and it fell to the floorboards. A shower of sparks erupted where it landed. His knees were weak. He suffocated on the cold and shadows.

Finnigan staggered beside him, as if the weight of the air was too much for him to stand again. He sank beside him, yet he still fought.

Finnigan reached for Flynn, catching him under the elbow. And with a great heave, Finnigan pulled him toward the stairs. They stumbled but started to gain traction and soon were skipping stairs. They tripped down the too-high risers, designed for persons far taller than they.

A roar caught their ears. The second floor crackled, the dry ancient wood of the floorboards had caught aflame. The embers had fallen to the floor covered in dust and caught fire with a rapid burst of heat. They could see the stairwell flare from the growing flames.

And the Dark, it came. A paced, measured, step by step, thud, thud, thud, down the stairs. A great ferocious beast of dark, of night, of the wild. Its eyes were two stones, glossy and deep, a perfect obsidian.

When Shadows Creep

It filled the staircase. Filled the room. It rose to full height and the top of the shadowy head brushed the ceiling. The floor creaked and groaned against its weight.

The sound of the storm outside blended with its snake-like hiss that came from deep within the creature.

Flynn and Finnigan backed away. Their exit to the wild snow was blocked by the great swing of long arms and the ferocious claws that adorned them.

"I'm so sorry Finnigan," Flynn whispered.

He wasn't certain Finnigan heard him over the roar of the fire and the bluster of the storm. Over the ever-present hiss of the creature that advanced on them. But Finnigan turned his head toward Flynn and gave a quiet nod. It was a nod that invoked far more understanding and knowledge than could ever be communicated with words.

The Darkness filled the room, every crevice and every knot, grown far greater than the space within this version of the Manor. It filled an overlap in existence, it filled beyond walls that were present. It heaved and swelled within the confines of reality.

"Flynn," the beast rumbled. When the creature spoke, it was a voice so low and loud that their teeth rattled in their jaws.

Flynn cringed and pressed against the stone wall next to the fireplace, bared to the Dark and its whim. There was no protection any longer.

"Let us grow," it growled as the floor burned away overhead.

Sparks and embers tumbled down around its head and shoulders. With a great creaking groan, one of the beams that ran the length of the room began to shift. The room heaved with a mighty rumble and part of the ceiling gave way to the floor below. It crashed down, thundering around the Darkness.

Finnigan was closer to the beast and acted as an ineffectual shield for Flynn. Debris fell over him, on his shoulder first, and he followed it to the floor and lay still.

Flynn cried out and tried to reach for Finnigan, but he was too far. Flynn couldn't know if he was still alive. His vision tunneled, the Manor around him fell away and all he could see was Finnigan's prone form on the floor.

The creature was the least of their problems as the Manor crumbled around them.

"I will never, ever help you! And I don't need this!"

Flynn pulled his hand from his pocket. The ebony stone glittered and swirled in his hand. He hurled it into the fireplace that flicked tongues of flames at his arms and legs.

It did not burn. No, not at first. It grew and twisted as melted, liquified glass rested in a nest of half-burnt logs and glowing charcoal. Then, the stone finally caught fire. It erupted into emerald flames and shrieked in a cacophony of cries that echoed over the heat and thunder of the blaze.

When Shadows Creep

The beast twisted as another crossbeam collapsed downward and crashed across its back. It screamed, long and loud, and the walls of the Manor throbbed with the reverberations. The Darkness caught fire as great tendrils of fire rippled across its shadowed form. Veins of liquid flame tore through the black, through the heart of it all.

Finnigan stirred, unaware of the thunder of the beast as it writhed over his head. Flynn chose the momentary distraction to crawl across the floor toward him. The heat was unbearable, and the floorboards erupted with every step. The entire Manor was ablaze, and Flynn wiped the sweat from his eyes. He finally reached Finnigan, his hands and knees blistered. It was a pain that screamed through him louder than any he'd ever felt.

He shook Finnigan by the shoulder. "Come on, Finnigan, we have to go, I destroyed it. Please. Wake up!"

Finnigan groaned and rolled toward him, looked up in a daze and blinked away his confusion. Grime and soot coated his face, and his sweat ran rivulets through it.

"I got you, Flynn, don't worry, don't you worry a bit." Finnigan's voice was thick and hoarse and he struggled to sit up. "We'll get out of this place."

Flynn's eyes were wild as he nodded, and then the Dark rose, writhing behind Finnigan's back.

Chapter Fourteen

Carmen

Carmen and Roman were stripped down to their shirt-sleeves. Their jackets were overwhelmingly hot in the combined brilliance of the sun and of the rolling waves of heat that were rolling off of Flynn and Finnigan's bodies.

"What do you think is happening? Where are they?" Carmen looked at Roman, incredulous.

Roman shook his head once more, as he'd done every time Carmen had asked this question over the past several hours.

But that was the truth. Time flowed differently in the undercurrent. It shuffled sideways and see-sawed forwards and backward in leaps and bounds. The flow of time, as unique as the space it flowed through, grew and shifted.

Carmen had once had the disturbing opportunity to witness this first hand. Carmen had returned from the undercurrent to discover that an entire year had passed, though only moments had passed within. Caden had been beside himself, unable to follow. He had been unlearned in the ways of the undercurrent, in blood magic, and knew of no way to retrieve Carmen from the beyond.

Thankfully, Carmen took steps to assure that it never happened again. Caden's ingrained reluctance to traverse through the membrane of reality had to take a backseat and he was given a crash course. They had been young then, and to Caden's happiness, it had never happened again.

Caden hovered over the brothers, his turn at the watch. The pair twitched and trembled, and Finnigan's hand ever tightened over Flynn's. It seemed as if he was afraid to lose the connection, afraid of Flynn being dropped in the cosmos and lost forever.

It was then, at that moment that the stone rolled from Flynn's hand, across his chest, and landed quietly in the notch between his chin and shoulder.

"Guys? You should come see this, he let it go," Caden said.

Carmen scrambled over to where they lay, Roman in quick pursuit.

"Dare you touch it?' Carmen looked to Roman with worry filled eyes.

Caden passed to him the handkerchief from his pocket, the same brilliant red as his jacket. Carmen didn't believe that it could possibly be enough to protect against the acidic nature of the Dark.

Roman's lips firmed into a straight, thin line as he concentrated. He wrapped the cloth tightly around his hand and fingers, took a deep breath and scooped up the stone. It was hot in his hand, far too hot and it rolled in his palm, almost danced and singed the cloth that protected his hand from the heat.

He turned toward Carmen, fear in his eyes. He outstretched his hand as the egg sat and glittered malevolently.

"How do we destroy it?" Carmen breathed, afraid to speak too loud, not wanting to disturb the concentrated evil in Roman's palm.

Caden knelt by Flynn and shook his shoulder. He pulled his hand back in pain. He blew on his fingers to quell the burn. "They're going to burn up, Carm, we got to get them inside, cool them down. I can barely touch him."

Carmen looked worriedly between Roman's hand and where the Freemonts lay. The statue stone steamed away the moisture from around their bodies.

"Give me that, take him," Carmen held out a hand to Roman, who wrapped the stone in the cloth and handed it off, then knelt by Caden's side.

Carmen headed up toward the house, the handkerchief held by the corners as a net for the stone, arm held out perfectly straight. It kept the egg as far away from touching skin or clothes as possible.

When Shadows Creep

. . .

Caden

Roman had one arm in his breaker, and looked up at Caden through his wild eyebrows. "Put your coat back on. It'll give a bit of protection from the heat. I'm afraid for where they are, what they're experiencing now. But you're right. We have to cool them. I don't know what will happen if we don't."

Despite his hundreds of years upon this earth, he was as strong as he had been as a young Guardian. He enjoyed employing the appearance of an old man, it made it useful with dealing with the humans. They either assumed him to be a kindly old man, or in extreme cases, were scared away by his grouchy old man demeanor. They worked when needed, but he always hid his strength. It was with this strength, that he tossed Finnigan over his shoulder with the finesse of an overlarge sack of flour, held him around the backs of his knees, and headed in the direction of the Manor.

Caden, after he donned his jacket, was a little more graceful and hauled Flynn up in a cradle. Flynn's head lolled against Caden's shoulder, his brow stitched in concern over events that Caden could only imagine.

"You're gonna have to come back, little guy. You got a lot of people worried about you and we need you to let us know you're okay."

201

The weight of Flynn burned in his arms, hot against his chest. He feared that Flynn would ignite, flare up, burn out hot and bright and disappear from his reach forever. Like a star, untouchable. His dogged pace soon caught up with Roman.

"Main floor? Are there any showers, bathtubs? I'm not sure how the Manor has configured in the last few hours, do we waste time trying to find them? What if the Manor won't let us in?" Caden's questions rolled off his tongue, an avalanche he could not control.

After hours of inaction and immobility, the only thought on his mind was that they were too late to do anything at all. Roman paused at the base of the wide sweeping staircase that led to the massive front doors and turned to stop Caden. "Maybe we don't have to think about any of that."

Caden turned to see where Roman had focused. The ground had slid into an alternate variation while they'd been down at the gates. Now, a spiral path broke off from where they stood, a river rock formation embedded thickly in the ground. It twisted off toward the back of the Manor, curled back at the halfway mark, around and around until it ended abruptly at a short dock and perfectly round pond.

"Oh Roman, no, we can't," Caden whined. But Roman had already headed down the pathway.

When Shadows Creep

He had shifted where Finnigan hung over his shoulder, and his head and arms bounced again Roman's back with every step. It turned out to be their best choice, for Caden and Roman had only made it two-thirds of the way around the circle before the heat became unbearable. Caden's hands blistered where they held Flynn.

"Drop them, just drop them, Caden, now!"

"But they'll drown."

"Caden, now!"

Roman had dipped down to one knee, had surveyed the mossy green water. It was cool and dark and clear, the pond lined in beautiful limestone. It looked to be several feet deep, and he had not hesitated as he rolled Finnigan off his shoulder, down, down into the water. Unable to resist the command, Caden knew that no matter what Roman would be right. He did as he was told. He dropped Flynn without ceremony into the water after Finnigan.

They both sank like stones. The water quickly drenched their clothes and pulled them down under the crystal clear water. Flynn's hair floated about his face.

Caden side-glanced at Roman, who had risen to his feet and stood with his arms crossed. He watched the bubbles rise to the surface as they sank to the bottom.

Caden's fingers flexed at his side. He itched to dive in, to retrieve them, to chastise Roman for this oversight.

"Calm, Caden. Wait."

Caden bore his gaze into the acidic green of Roman's eyes. Without a break in eye contact, Caden shook his head. He began to strip off his coat and his button-up shirt. He hopped on one foot, then the other as he pulled off his heavy boots. He prepared himself to reclaim the Freemonts.

Roman held out a warning hand. "Wait."

...

Flynn

The wind whipped through the holes in the collapsed roof. Ice and snow pelted Flynn's skin in a ferocious rush. He gasped at the sudden and intense cold. Finnigan struggled with the same staggered rush to his system, groping across the floor for Flynn's hand.

Their fingers entwined, cold and brittle, scoured by the flames and the ice, blistered from the heat. The agony of this one action was enough to center Flynn. It aligned their thoughts, Freemont to Freemont, and Finnigan squeezed.

It was an invisible hand that gripped the base of the spine and the nape of the neck. It was a cruel claw that pulled and pulled, the sensation of the world being ripped from under their feet. It was the nothingness of the spaces between the walls of reality, the Dark, the taste of iron and copper of blood. Around and around and upside down, until it no longer mattered which way was which. It only mattered that there was a way, and that it was the path to take.

Flynn's focus and feeling and entire scope of his existence depended on the warmth of the contact of Finnigan's palm and nothing else.

Nothing.

The pronounced sound of one single heartbeat echoed in his ears. And then the abrupt and panicked sensation of being dropped from an unexpected height, the flip of a stomach, and they were underwater.

Flynn's eyes flew open. His sudden intake of air caused him to choke and he kicked, kicked, he swam, toward the brilliant blue sapphire of the sky above. Or below. He couldn't tell, he was so disoriented by the sudden cold and weightlessness. His clothes weighed him down and he resisted the urge to scream because then he would drown. He would drown.

These thoughts tumbled through his head as quickly as the cascade in his brain could trawl them up from the depths that created them. He saw a hand. There was a hand and he urged every fiber of his being to grab, to take, to reach, and he took it. Then his head was free and there was air and he choked as he was hauled up onto the rocks.

Finnigan was flopped soggy beside him, his face to the stones. He coughed up water exhumed from deep within, took a deep breath and rolled onto his side. The look on his face was one of relief and awe and hysterical laughter unbroken from his chest.

Caden grabbed Flynn by the shoulder, rolled him onto his back and shook him until Flynn's teeth rattled in his jaw. "What the Hell, Flynn?"

Caden put his forehead in his hands then rolled to the ground beside them.

Roman looked down, amusement sparkling in his eyes. His hands were shoved in his pockets and his jaw that tick-ticked away as he bit back the words he wanted to say. Without warning, though, his demeanor shifted. His shoulders hunched, his eyes clouded over and his head snapped up toward the Manor.

"You destroyed it, Flynn, you destroyed it in the undercurrent?"

Flynn frowned. His head was still spinning and his was still drawing in slow breaths in gasps. He processed what Roman said, and nodded.

Caden had already rolled to his feet, had attempted to throw his shirt back on. It was inside out and buttoned half way but fully askew, and he took off toward the Manor. He leaped in great bounds from path to path until he hit the gravel of the curved driveway and picked up speed.

Flynn rolled toward Finnigan in confusion and looked for an explanation from his brother, but Finnigan had also scrambled to his feet. He had already headed toward the Manor as fast as his soggy clothes would allow.

When Shadows Creep

Flynn's teeth chattered and his shoulders rocked with convulsions. He wavered as he tried to stand, took a deep breath, and then followed them. Pebbles and grit and leaves attached themselves to his socks with every step.

Something was wrong.

Smoke curled from the rooftop of the Manor, where no chimney or stovepipe poked through the frost covered shingles. It was black and billowed, catching in the brisk wind that whipped off the fields and ruffled the gold of the surrounding trees.

The Manor was on fire.

Flynn hobbled along. His eyes began to water; the acrid smoke had switched directions and blew into his face. It smelled like no other smoke. It was the expected scent of wood and asphalt, but something else was there, just underneath it. Pine and storms and the sea, the smell of green loam that whipped off the waves when the algae bloomed. It was thick, cloying and invasive. It crawled into his nose and mouth and lungs and he could taste every cloud that twisted his way.

The other three hadn't even gotten as far as the front door before the Manor twisted about. They had run up the staircase and a shuffle of neatly trimmed topiaries engulfed them and deposited them swiftly inside.

The Manor was panicking. Flynn could see where the rooms had pushed outward, away from the blaze. The façade rippled through alternates like a deck of cards. The Manor reached desperately for a version of itself where it was no longer on fire.

But it wasn't to be.

The Darkness had caught alight in that cold and cursed place. On the coattails of Flynn and Finnigan's return to this reality, the dark and the flames had thrummed along through the webbing with them. The Dark churned with fire and had caught the core of the Manor aflame through and through.

Flynn had no more reached the top of the entrance stairs when he staggered. He petered on the edge of a step that was now inside, at the top of the staircase that faced the chandelier. The room and the hallways were filled with thick black smoke. Flynn flung an arm over his face and dropped to the floor, coughing hard. He flung an arm over his face and tried to find a way beneath the smoke. The Manor had dropped him here for some reason. The source of the fire must be nearby.

An enraged scream pierced through the blackness, echoed through the hallways and bounced along the ceiling. The chandelier rattled with the force of it. Thousands of crystals shuddered and shivered, tinkling through destruction. And then the chandelier fell.

Flynn watched, horrified. The grand chandelier teetered for a moment on the edge of here and then, existence and not, then it crashed to the ground in an ear-splitting cacophony. Shattered crystals scattered in every direction, the floor frosted in their obliteration.

The roof over Flynn's head was ablaze, fingertips of fire crawling along the edges of the plaster. They clawed their way down to the walls like a living thing of evil and anger and retribution.

Flynn turned away, toward the other end of the hallway he was crouched in and began to crawl, slow and beleaguered. He was dragged down by his almost inability to breath and the damp of his sweater. He had to find the others. Carmen had been long gone when he'd returned, and now everyone was gone, somewhere inside. The Dark... it had followed them, and it was going to lay waste to the Manor for Flynn's insolence and betrayal.

What have I done?

The words screamed in Flynn's head, over and over. Each time a blow, punishment for his crimes against the Guardians.

A thunderous crash came from behind where he crawled, and he moved faster. He could hear voices, but he wasn't sure where they were coming from. The crackle of the rushing flames distorted other sounds and prevented him from hearing clearly. He could have sworn it was Finnigan's voice.

Up ahead, Finnigan's face peered around the crossroads of the hallways, soot-stained and hair plastered to his head. Here, the smoke was lighter, still high against the ceiling. It was less likely to choke and maim, but still dangerous and as it billowed.

"Nothing like out of the frying pan and then, again, into the frying pan, right Flynn?"

Flynn coughed in agreement and slumped against the corner of his hall. He was shoulder to shoulder with Finnigan, who held his damp sleeve over his mouth.

"Where is everyone?" Flynn asked before he followed suit and held his collar over his face. It provided brief, almost non-existent relief from the smoke as he rested.

"The Manor separated us when it pulled us all in. I've no idea where anyone is. The last thing Caden said to me was that Carmen had entered the Manor with the egg shortly before we returned. Presumably to destroy it."

"But *we* destroyed it, in the undercurrent, in the fire, it was gone. I burned it, it disappeared." Flynn's steady reassurance through his rambling commentary did little to hide his panic. If Carmen had the stone, the darkness would soon follow.

It would know. It would know that the stone was here too.

Flynn's heart skipped a beat. There was a stone here too. And it knew. The Dark knew. Finnigan grabbed Flynn's bony knee where it rested near his hand and squeezed it hard. It pulled Flynn back from the edge.

"Hey. It's like us, right? There was us, here, our bodies, and us, there, in the undercurrent. It's the same with the stone, alright? We have to destroy both, both of the stones, and then it'll be gone for good, okay? We've got this." Finnigan's voice was low and meant to soothe, for once, as he said all the right things and at the exactly right moment.

But Flynn knew this was a lie. They were as good as trapped, unable to see, unable to flee, unable to find the others. Flynn began gulping down air, and clenching his fists, as he stared a hole into the ceiling. He needed to be here. He needed to be present until this was over. In the quiet moment, another beam crashed down and blocked off their exit to the staircase.

"The Manor is going to come down around us, it can't shift past this, Finnigan. It's done. Can't you feel it?"

Flynn reached a trembling hand and placed it on the wall, searched hard for the thud of the heartbeat that should have been strong against his palm. Nothing but warm plaster, no life left behind the walls.

Finnigan's back rested against the wall, his shoulders hunched, and he made no move to touch the Manor. He knew. Flynn could tell by the look on his face that he had known it even as he said it.

The smoke thickened around them, rolled through in a dark haze that removed all visibility and scorched at their eyes and their skin.

Finnigan's grip tightened on Flynn's knee. His voice, hoarse and strained, no more than a whisper near Flynn's ear. "Flynn, I can't see, I can't see anything at all."

Flynn had squeezed his eyes shut, tight against the smoke. Tight against the tears that wanted to form against the hopelessness in Finnigan's voice.

And then a thought. *Maybe...*

Flynn opened his eye, the one touched by the Darkness and the evil and the cold that had blossomed under his hand, and he *could see*. The fire wasn't of this world but created in another. The smoldering ruins of another reality had poured into theirs, and caught it ablaze, and it meant that *he could see*. The Dark had made him something new, something different. His eye could see through this smoke as clearly as he had seen the darkness within Finnigan and he would use this to his advantage.

Flynn reached for Finnigan's hand and pulled him up to a crouch. A quick survey of their surroundings showed that the hall that Finnigan had crawled down was not blocked, but continued along past two more crossroads.

Flynn dragged Finnigan toward what he hoped was their salvation.

When Shadows Creep

Carmen

Carmen slammed the door in the face of the creature advancing along the corridor, part smoke and part darkness.

And evidently, all evil.

Enraged, a great howl issued from its mouth as its edges wreathed in flame and everything caught fire in its path. Beautiful portraits of ancestors were long gone. Velvet curtains, tapestries, carpet runners. Furniture older than time remembered, disintegrated or burned beyond repair.

Carmen palmed the doorknob, begged for an alternate route, a shift toward a room on the outer edges of the Manor. An escape route of any sort. But the Manor would not respond, its existence in tatters, the magic now gone. The stone in Carmen's pocket was ice-cold. Carmen couldn't quite understand if that was a good thing or a painful indication of the things to come.

The door thudded, rocked in its frame and cracks of firelight flickered around the edges. The Darkness would get in and it would get its stone— its egg, its seed, *whatever* it was— and it would kill Carmen in the process. Carmen was sure of it.

The wallpaper bubbled and flared into black splotches of extinguished flame and soot. The growth bloomed like a mold across the walls. It spread, dark and malignant across the blue-sprigged walls.

Carmen realized, then, which room had been lurking at the end of the hall. Which room the Darkness had herded everyone to when they had entered the Manor. It was the room that Flynn built; recovered and restored to its former glory in the Freemont House. And it was evident now that this was where the Darkness would make its final stand.

If Roman was right, and the Dark needed only Flynn to wreak the havoc it so desired, nothing except Flynn would be good enough. It was charging through, rampaging across the Manor and destroying everything that had meant anything to the Guardians. The Dark would not try to bargain. It would not leave the Manor alone, it would not leave it to be rebuilt. Carmen knew if they handed over Flynn that would be it. It would be the end. And Carmen knew that Flynn would go to it, would do anything to save the Guardians and the Manor from this fiery demise.

Carmen wouldn't let him do it.

It was their home, their safe space, their grounding point, their responsibility. But all of that paled in comparison to their duty to the world, the undercurrent, and the multiverse.

And this was where the Dark had made an error. It misunderstood their connection with the Manor.

When Shadows Creep

All of the Guardians would let it burn. Burn to ash and nothingness, erased from the existence of every time and place if it meant that this darkness could be stopped.

Carmen hadn't had the chance to find out if Flynn and Finnigan had destroyed the egg in the undercurrent, hadn't had the chance to even ask how it would be done. But it would have to be done.

And Roman was somewhere, unreachable within the Manor, maybe alive, maybe dead.

Carmen's heart raced, the flood of confusion was overwhelming and tears began to flow.

I need Roman. I need to know what to do.

A few steadying breaths later, Carmen focused again on the wall.

Deep breath in.

Deep breath out.

Carmen pressed against the far wall, back against the window. Outside, the day was untouched by the Darkness and the devastation within, the sky brilliant as the sun streamed.

Carmen could feel the heat from the window, the coolness of the glass. The door rattled once again, buckled against latch and hinges, bowed by the beast on the other side. The thunderous boom of its attempts to enter were all but deafening.

A normal door would have been destroyed by now, splintered into thousands of pieces. But the Manor apparently still had a few secrets left in its dying grasp, and it would use it to protect the Guardians. Another door, in another wall, on the far side of the room staggered into view. It flickered in and out of existence, once, twice, and then faded. Carmen ran for it, but the knob disappeared before it could be touched.

Carmen's hope died with it.

Carmen struggled with the sense of loss. It was all around, filling the air. The desperation was thicker than the smoke.

The Dark needed to get in. The Manor wouldn't let it. The cosmic tug-of-war manifested in the rumblings and the rubble, the flicker of the lights and the shudder of the floor. The entire hardwood floor heaved and then tilted to a thirty-degree angle. The furniture slid and the rocking horse tumbled and Carmen stumbled along with it. Everything, lamps, couches, artwork, all crushed against the far wall like a ship in a storm. The stone had slipped from Carmen's pocket in the tumble, lost somewhere amongst the debris.

Carmen scrambled as the door burst open and the Darkness exploded inward. Great obsidian claws dragged it along the floor as the smoke twisted around it in heavy wreaths and the eyes glinted in a midnight face.

When Shadows Creep

"Give it to me," the floor rumbled with the voice. The walls shook and dust began to fall from the ceiling, and plaster snowed down on Carmen's head.

"You're never going to get it. We will never let you use it, never," Carmen yelled over the din.

The Dark smiled, revealing enormous fangs that glinted like daggers between its lips. The overwhelming scent of wet sand and ocean foam cascaded from its gaping maw. Carmen held back a wave of sickness that threatened to erupt in response, and tried to look for a weapon amongst the scattered pieces of the former room.

The Darkness approached and laughed. It grew as the destruction of the Manor fueled the power of its malice, greater and greater. A portion of the wall behind Carmen buckled and collapsed downward and took the sofa with it.

Carmen wavered, hands desperate for support from something, anything. But nothing could be found, and Carmen fell into the hole after it, into the next room, and onto the sofa.

Caden was there. He extended his hand and pulled Carmen up to standing. He was covered head-to-toe in soot and smears, his clothes in tatters around him as he stood barefoot on the carpet.

"Where is it?" Caden's eyes were frantic.

Carmen gestured toward the debris and they both lunged toward the ever-growing collection of rubble. Caden began to fling the shattered pieces of flotsam in all directions trying to dig out the egg before the Dark found it.

The room Carmen had emerged from, where the Dark had last been seen, was now strangely silent. The Darkness had not followed through when the wall collapsed, and neither of them had any idea where it now lurked.

Caden's shoulders were hunched, his hands desperate as he grasped at a table, three of the four legs broken. A dislodged blue and white china vase turned. Something rattled inside it. He flung the table away.

Carmen scooped the vase from the floor and turned it over Caden's waiting hand. The stone rattled ominously before it dropped. It glittered innocently in his hand. The Darkness swirled under a layer of frost glazed on its surface.

"How'd they destroy it?" Carmen asked with bated breath, unable to think.

This day had become an exercise in complete and utter exhaustion. It showed in their dark eyes and the circles beneath them. Caden slung an arm around Carmen's neck, to give and receive support, and they swayed in their tiredness. It was only a moment, only one, to take a breath before he continued. "Fire."

Carmen gaped after Caden as he wiped soot from his brow and headed toward the door. His feet slid as he climbed. He pressed an ear to the wood, listening for a sign of the Dark.

When Shadows Creep

The Manor creaked around them and lurched once more. The Caldwells staggered, but maintained their footing. Caden pulled the door open a mere inch and looked out into the smoke-filled hallway. He coughed, the air heavy in his lungs.

"What do you mean, fire?" Carmen whispered urgently in Caden's ear.

Caden turned and stared at Carmen for a moment, lips pursed, then continued. "He threw it in the fire."

"We're surrounded by fire! Are you telling me we could be done with it that easily?"

Caden had opened the door a little farther, his head outside of the room. He looked up and down both directions of the hall then pulled himself back in and closed the door quietly behind him. He pressed his back against the shut door.

"It's that easy if we can do it without the Dark noticing, scooping up the egg, and running off with it to perform its dastardly deeds."

Carmen's eyes rolled. "So we need to distract it? You go one way, I go the other?"

"Carm, it's not that easy. We can't have one of us dead for the trouble."

"It means the *end of existence* if it succeeds, Caden! You've got to believe that it'd be worth it."

They'd begun to hiss their words in their frustration, their urge to remain hidden mingling with their desperate attempts to win the argument.

Caden's jaw ticked, the muscle flexing in a hard spasm as he bit back his words.

Carmen swallowed hard, eyes searching Caden's for any sign that he'd accept the responsibility. That everything, absolutely everything, depended on their success.

"I hate you," Caden shook his head and dipped it backward against the door. His eyes focused on the twisted and bent ceiling over their heads.

Carmen remained silent.

"Bait or burn?" Caden asked. He had withdrawn a coin from his pocket, large and silver and engraved with the head of a gorgon. His lucky coin. He balanced it on thumb and finger, made it flick up into the air.

Carmen wasn't going to let him leave it to chance, and snatched the coin out of the air, pocketing it.

Caden had only half a moment to complain before Carmen slipped past him, opened the door, and with only a brief touch to his shoulder in passing, whispered back, "I call bait."

Carmen retreated from their hiding place leaving Caden staring after. There was no time for formalities. The Guardians had to put an end to the Dark. Carmen needed

When Shadows Creep

a way to pull the Dark far enough away so Caden could destroy the stone.

A small part of Carmen begged for him to call out to insist that they fight this together, or not at all. Begged him to insist they leave this place, leave the Manor, strike up where they could, hide wherever they could and never return.

But Carmen was determined to be far braver than ever before.

Chapter Fifteen

Roman

Roman had found the trapdoor to the armory. It was buried beneath the cascade of glass that had once been the atrium ceiling. It had come down during one of the violent quakes that rocked the Manor. With only a few minor cuts to his hands and ankles, he'd uncovered the entrance and descended into a terrible decision.

With the Manor as unstable as it was, it was likely a death trap to crawl his way underground in search of the weapons. But what more could he do? They weren't going to win by battling wits. And they certainly weren't going to win by scurrying room to room, playing a deadly game of hide and seek with a creature older than time.

Roman paused as a screeching roar echoed through the corridors and rattled the glass across the concrete floor overhead. He stepped softly, and picked his way through the darkness with care. His hand flitted across silver and iron, jagged things that could prick and slice with one wrong touch. He'd set this room up himself, so long ago it was beyond his memory, but he came here often to reminisce.

The Guardians of these days had rarely needed what this room held. But the habits of the old guard were always there in the back of his mind; a bitter reminder of what could happen if he slackened his attention. There were those who took advantage of the worn out and thin places between realities. Those who, with enough power, could break through to wreak havoc on unsuspecting universes.

His hand came to rest on a curve of polished wood, smooth beneath his hand. A ripple of thrill ran through him, electrifying his nerve endings.

Fire is the answer.

Flynn had proven that with the stone. He had destroyed a piece of the beast, the Darkness. Despite how it raged and rampaged through the Manor, Roman knew that the fire that wreathed its form would eventually destroy it. Its search for the stone was made all the more desperate by its imminent demise.

It just happened to be taking the rest of the Manor down with it.

"This will help it along, to wherever creatures like this go when they die," Roman muttered.

He pulled the heavy object out of its holder fastened to the wall then moved back toward the patch of sunlight filtering down into the hatch and inspected the weapon.

It was a thing of beauty, his crossbow. Made from the wood of trees that no longer existed, in a reality that had long ago collapsed. He treasured it, its accuracy, and the solid feeling of security it lent him. This weapon had survived the destruction of its home world, and it would live to protect this one.

Roman returned into the darkness to search for the quiver that held the bolts. It was an easy find when faced with his rabid attention to organization.

In short order, Roman had returned to the hatch, clambered out of the hole and begun his path toward the library. He hoped the Manor hadn't dispatched it elsewhere. The fear of the whole collection catching flame would be enough for the House to ensure that the library would be one of the first rooms to shift away. But he could feel the quiet below the crash and roar of destruction in the other rooms. He could feel the stillness in the air that indicated the Manor was gone.

Roman felt the loss deep in his gut, akin to the loss of a limb. He'd been here so long, the Manor was an extension of himself and who he was. And now it was gone. Just like that. Just another building in the sweep of the country that marched forward in ignorance of the chain of universes that existed around it.

The floor swayed, as the whole house beneath his feet tried to heave itself out of the ground, to shake loose the beast within. Roman slid down the tile, his dress shoes without grip. He leaned away from his descent to control the slide down the corridor. He crouched when he hit the wall at the end beneath his feet and covered his head from the deluge of furniture and artwork that rained down. When the avalanche ceased, only papers left fluttering around his feet, he leapt up and continued on.

The angle of the twist of the Manor meant he was running along the wall. He leapt across doorways and searched his memory for the exact door that would lead him into the library.

It wasn't books he looked for, though. It was the alcohol in the extensive bar Finnigan kept. A wide variety of what Roman felt may have been every distilled beverage known to mankind was stored there. He smiled wryly to himself. If he was lucky, there'd be more than a few bottles left unbroken by the upheaval. He'd use the alcohol as a substitute fuel for his flaming arrows, to send the Darkness so much light and heat that it was vanquished.

He pictured in his head the great wall of bottles, shelf above shelf above shelf, accessed by an increasingly rickety ladder as one climbed. Each bottle was carefully under-lit so as to make the wall glitter like a thousand gemstones.

Roman couldn't count the number of times Finnigan had fallen from that ladder in an insane attempt to reach for an acquisition that the others had long forgotten. It was always for the "perfect" accompaniment to whatever strange dish he'd decided to serve up that day.

He leapt over one final door and then paused, looking around at the décor, or what remained of it. He backed up to the previous entrance. Within, the library had twisted in an opposing direction. It appeared as if the entire house had been wrung like a wet cloth, and the black and white tiled floor met the door frame at a bizarre upward angle. Roman's mind spun with the thought of the exterior of the Manor and how it might look to an outsider or casual passerby; a crumpled piece of paper made of mortar and brick and shingles, smoke-filled and on fire. He'd have to deal with the fall out later.

Maybe the entire Manor would burn down to ash and he'd never have to craft a believable lie for a demolition team to raze what remained.

The thought hurt too much.

But this angle of the library meant that the bar was mainly safe. The bottles had only slid to the far side of their respective shelves, cradled by their custom shelving, safe from breakage. This world was his oyster, he just needed the perfect pearl to execute his plan.

That bastard would burn.

When Shadows Creep

. . .

Flynn

Flynn had finally found a room that was clear of smoke and relatively unharmed by the flex of the Manor. The room had been rounded, curved and bent about an unseen space. It appeared to Flynn the same as a car that had careened into a telephone pole, the engine bowed. Every object in the room had piled high into one corner. A couch balanced on a chair here, a table balanced on an ottoman there.

Finnigan wheezed, his lungs constricted and raw from the smoke, and he leaned hard against the wall.

"How haven't we found anyone?" Finnigan choked.

Flynn wiped his mouth with the back of his hand, returned it black from soot into his pocket. He shook his head. He ran to the window, tried to yank it open. He needed air. He was becoming claustrophobic in this crumpled version of the Manor. No walls were straight, no rooms were square. It played with his head and he felt small. He guessed that more than half of the House had gone up in flame. It was no small wonder that they'd found this oasis.

"I wish I knew what the others were doing. What was Roman's plan? If we're better off outside than in here? What if the house collapses?"

Finnigan considered an answer, stifled a deep cough that tried to fight its way free, and shook his head. "There's no if, Flynn. The Manor is going to come down. And we aren't going to want to be in it when it does." Finnigan slid to the ground, his head in his hands.

Flynn had managed to crack the window. The cool breeze flowed over him, and he took deep gulps of the fresh air. "What happens if it collapses?" He asked between deep breaths.

"Well, if it collapses, it means all of it has succumbed, right through every single variation. It leaves an absence in the space, throughout reality, throughout the undercurrent. It doesn't just collapse. It implodes and leaves a gap in everything and then reality crumbles around it. There won't be a soft spot anymore. It'll just be rubble." Finnigan stared out into space, unseeing with a soft twist to his mouth that denoted an unknown horror that he couldn't quite process.

Flynn froze for a moment, as the possibility of it all swooped through his mind. He licked his lips furtively, the taste of salt and ash on his skin. He chewed his cheek for a moment. "And what happens if we are inside when that happens?"

Finnigan's response was delayed. He startled as if he had been lost in thought. He looked up where Flynn was braced against the window, silhouetted against the light. "Do you really have to ask?"

Flynn hunched over in response and the window at his back became much more than just a spot to lean. It was the only thing that kept him from a collapse straight down to the ground.

"I can't believe I did this," Flynn said. He stared up at the ceiling and shook his head, the words quiet against the rumble of the blaze that slowly ate away at the Manor.

"You couldn't have known Flynn, you can't blame yourself."

Flynn's eyes bored into Finnigan's, a challenge to prove that he was wrong. Finnigan couldn't— *wouldn't*— rise to the bait, and broke the eye contact before Flynn could comment once more.

"Once we defeat this, I- I'll return to Freemont House. The Dark won't be there any longer. It will be fine. I will leave you all alone. Stop ruining your lives and your livelihood." Flynn swallowed hard and sank to the floor. The two brothers faced each other across the carpet, thick with plaster dust from the shattered ceiling.

Finnigan let out a strange noise and Flynn looked up, brow knitted.

"Are you... are you laughing, Finnigan?"

Finnigan shook his head, but his mouth cracked into a grin, and a hysterical titter escaped his lips. He brushed both hands through his hair and the motion sent dust and ash into the air around his head. His hair had become almost as white as Flynn's from the filth.

"Finnigan, what?"

"Flynn, if we defeat this, the Manor is done. We'll have to come live with you. There's nowhere else for us to go."

Flynn wiped his nose and stared at the floor to consider the possibility. They *would* have to, he realized that now. The Guardians would have to move into Freemont House to survive if the Manor was truly destroyed. They had no choice. His eyes returned to Finnigan's and he realized that Finnigan stared at him.

"You won't get rid of us that easily, Flynn. It's all together now." Finnigan's broad, white smile was genuine, and Flynn returned it, despite the utter panic that raced around his mind. He would take this moment, wrap it up safely, and keep it deep down inside for those moments when it all became too much.

Flynn drummed at his knees, and his fingers left white marks in the damp fabric. "So where do we go from here?"

...

Caden

Carmen's voice traveled down the hall, loud and strong, taunting the Darkness. Caden smiled for a moment as he pinned himself against the door frame to the room they'd taken refuge in, the stone frozen in his hand.

He needed to find the heart of the blaze, the place where the Dark had come through from the undercurrent when it followed Flynn and Finnigan. There, the fire would be the white-hot blaze of destruction, there he would find the hottest coals. The stone would be destroyed instantly and they could leave the Manor to its ruin.

Streamers of darkness separated themselves from the smoke that billowed along that hallway. Pieces of the Dark melded into an angry seething mass that moved like a tidal wave towards Carmen's voice. The vacuum left behind by the creature swirled the smoke into a ripple of heat and ash. It flowed like a river down the corridor in the direction in which it moved.

Caden stepped out onto the buckled floor, tentative at first, trying not to make a sound. He didn't know if it could sense the seed, if it had any sort of extrasensory link to the piece of itself that it had left behind. He didn't want to find out before he'd tossed it to its demise, either.

A cool, clean breeze flirted with his face as he ran down the hall toward the remains of the staircase. He'd been drowning in the thick atmosphere, and he welcomed the air.

He stopped dead and tilted his face toward the direction of the flowing air and noticed the brightness of the corridor he had just passed. He walked back a few steps and gaped at what he saw.

It was as if a massive bite had been taken out of the Manor. The hallway he stared down abruptly ended at a jagged chasm. The bright October sunlight glittered all around, the sky blindingly blue after the dark of the besieged House. He stood at the edge and looked down and he blanched.

A slow eddy swirled below with detritus from the Manor screeching and squealing as large chunks collided and spun down. It was a painfully slow drain into an unknown vortex. The collapse had already begun, and reality had reclaimed what no longer belonged.

Across from where he stood, the remainder of the hallway still hung from a partially collapsed stone wall, the roof fully engulfed in flames, the section of Manor beyond unrecognizable. A time cap had just been placed neatly on top of Caden's mission. Once the stone was destroyed, he'd have to find and get everyone out safely, or they'd be lost forever.

A stream of expletives passed his lips and he turned back to the hall from which he'd come. An eerie silence reigned over the dust that settled to the ground. He could no longer hear Carmen, nor the angry roar of the Darkness. Caden pressed to the wall, wary of a trap. He was too exposed here.

A crack began to fissure at the baseboard, a dark crunch of a snap that worked its way, slow and jagged, up toward the ceiling. It bypassed a mirror that had miraculously stayed affixed to the wall, the ornate frame a burnished gold in the brightness of the light. Caden's eyes followed the scar in the wall until he realized what it meant.

The corridor he stood in was next to go, and it would soon collapse into the vortex he'd left not too far behind.

Caden ran.

He didn't look back, even when he heard the resounding cannon-like boom. The boom that announced that the part of the Manor he'd just taken refuge in had thundered down into the chasm with the rest of the House.

The room of the central staircase loomed up ahead, completely dark except for the flicker of flame. He thought he'd heard the chandelier fall soon after they'd been thrown askew into the Manor. Part of him had hoped that it wasn't true.

Despite his tentative association with it over the past day, he'd always loved the chandelier. It was a beautiful work of art that centered the energy and emotion of the Manor and seemed to operate as a tether for all of the Guardians. It had been the room to which they'd always magnetically drifted, the beginning and end of every journey.

This was truly the end of the journey. The Manor wasn't coming back from this.

Caden paused at the doorway and assessed the room. Unbearable heat poured from the east corridor, an inferno that wavered at the edge of the staircase. The tongues of flame licked the stairs and had turned the wrought iron railings white-hot. He covered his face with his arm and tried to peer through to the other side. The stone began to rattle in his pocket, a high-pitched vibrato that thrummed against his chest.

"You don't like that, do you?"

Caden glared down at his pocket and continued into the chamber. He had to be headed in the right direction, the warning sound was all he needed for proof.

He carefully made his way around the staircase, tried to avoid the firefly embers of glowing ash that fluttered down around him. They singed his clothes where they touched.

A mighty roar shook the room and the ground shuddered under his feet in a heartbeat thud of giant footsteps.

"Caden!" Carmen's scream surged through the room and Caden turned, a moment too late.

"Give me what is mine. No more silly games." The Dark heaved, the entirety of its form rose and fell with unconstrained anger, pacing through the sharp glass that whirled at its feet.

The Dark landed a swift uppercut to his jaw and he flew across the room, over the glittering shards of chandelier. He landed against the wall at the top of the stairs, thudded against the plaster and collapsed through the drywall.

When Shadows Creep

...

Carmen

"Give me what is mine, no more silly games."

The fragments of crystals from the ruined chandelier rumbled across the ground with the depth of the monster's voice. Fist-sized chunks of the ceiling rained down around it and Carmen, who held ground at the bottom of the stairs.

It approached Carmen with its massive teeth bared and its claws unsheathed. Its current form was that of a great burly panther, darker than dark, the ripple of fur and hide and smoke deep over its muscular form.

Carmen was weaponless aside from a small knife, and the despair of certain doom crept through Carmen's chest like a rising flood.

The creature bundled down upon itself, every muscle poised to leap, to strike, to take Carmen down with a single blow on its way to destroy Caden.

A piercing whistle shot through the air, as vivid as a lightning bolt, and the creature froze. Carmen's eyes shot in the direction of the sound.

Roman stood on the balcony over the flame, crossbow in hand. A flaming bolt was locked and loaded, aimed square at the beast's back.

With a crackle, the bolt flew in an arc of fire, a shooting star through the air of the chamber, and plunged into the shoulder of the monstrous shape. The Dark arched its back and writhed.

Flynn came up from the left, then, and brandished a jar full of bolts, tied up with strips of cloth. They sat in a large blue bottle that Carmen recognized as the strongest proof vodka in Finnigan's stash. Roman loaded up the crossbow and Finnigan approached from the opposite side with a lighter and ignited the cloth into a fiery blue ball. Roman shot into the advancing darkness.

They proceeded in this fashion, over and over lightning fast as the creature approached with roars of pain and anger. It began to climb the wall toward them, away from where Caden fell. Its enormous claws skewered the wall and it climbed gecko-like to the top floor. The Dark curved around the entry way, and its massive head peered down into the hallway.

Roman paused, waiting for the next bolt to be loaded. Flynn's hands were empty, though, and he shook his head.

They were out of ammunition. And still, the beast came.

Flynn threw the bottle of vodka at the Darkness' head. It shattered into pieces and showered the Dark and the surroundings in alcohol. The beast charged.

"Watch out!" Carmen shrieked.

When Shadows Creep

Roman snatched the lighter from Finnigan's hand and snapped it open, once, twice, but the flint refused to catch the wick. The lighter was dead.

Carmen watched as they ducked in unison and rolled to the sides of the hall. The creature stampeded forward like a bull or a train, a force beyond reckon.

The whoosh of air and smoke should have stunned them, but they moved as the swipe of its claws raked great slices into the walls and the floor. The trio changed direction and ran back toward the staircase. They avoided the spots in the floor where the fire had burned away right up through the floorboards. The walls and carpet had begun to ignite from the heat below and several spots in the floor were burned all the way through the floorboards. It was a tunnel of fire.

The ground shattered beneath their feet as they ran, always a moment too quick for the floor to catch their ankles. Ahead of them, Caden had climbed free of the hole in the wall and waited for the other three to reach him.

. . .

Caden

The beast filled the entire corridor from wall to wall, ceiling to floor, a great mass of darkness like a starless void and tried to chase them down. The ceiling above Caden's

237

head had caught fire and the massive beams that had held the chandelier were finally aflame and looked like they could collapse at any moment.

"You're going to have to jump!" Caden yelled over the roar of beast and flame alike, more forceful than he ever had been, or ever would be.

The three leaped to the railing and time seemed to stop. They paused for a moment with their feet on the banister. Their arms were waving, their knees wobbling. But a half glance behind at the hell that followed them was enough, and they leapt toward Caden.

Caden wound up his arm, egg clutched in his hand, and he waited for his moment.

The Dark lunged one last time and paused at the entrance to the room. It stared at Caden with eyes so dark they disappeared into the smoke. It stared at the egg he held in his hand and began to laugh. The walls shook with the sound, and the Manor responded with a great shudder.

Caden threw the egg directly into the Darkness, a straight shot into its mouth. The Darkness shut its great fanged mouth, closed its teeth tight over the egg and brandished a horrible smile that made Caden's skin crawl.

And that's when the beam fell. Broken from a crossbeam, it swung directly toward the creature.

The Manor would have the last laugh.

When Shadows Creep

The massive wooden beam as thick as a tree trunk, in a burst of flame, hit the Darkness square in the mouth. The vodka ignited in a flash of fire and the creature began to scream. It clawed at its face, raking massive gouges into its face and skin and arms trying to scratch away the flame. It reared back, half horse, half lion, and collapsed backward onto the floor.

The floor, seared and destroyed as it had been from the east corridor below, could not hold the weight of the collapsed dark and its energy. The hallway buckled, the wood splintered, and the second floor disintegrated, taking the Dark with it.

Flynn, Finnigan, and Roman gaped from the floor of the central chamber. They stared at the flames enveloping the shrieking beast where it writhed and glowed with the ferocious heat.

Caden watched from his spot at the top of the stairs, as the remainder the Manor began to crack. Massive fissures rose up the walls and bisected the floor, and the entire House began to heave. It tipped toward where the vortex swirled on the east side of the Manor.

Like an iceberg being calved, the east side of the chamber separated from west and the east end sank, with the monster. The floor tipped toward oblivion and burst into a thousand pieces.

Caden descended the stairs and groped for Carmen's arm. The pair, in turn, scooped up the others, under arms, by hands, connected. They supported each other as they limped, bruised and sooty and near exhaustion, out of the front doors of the Manor for one last time.

Chapter Sixteen

They'd crossed the boundary to the rest of the world then turned back to watch. Here they were guaranteed to be safe, away from the thin place in time and space that was now slowly sinking. It was a great ship in a sea of disbelief. None of the Guardians were concerned about cars that may have passed on the road; cars that may have slowed, concerned for the ragtag group that stood wild-eyed outside of a ramshackle gate.

All their eyes were focused on the final moments of the Manor, on the raw energy of what was collapsing around them.

Flynn and Finnigan had had it easy. When their responsibility for the playground had come to an end, it had simply disappeared into the night.

It simply never came home again.

But for the others, this was a raw and painful death. The death throes of the Manor and the shriek of the universe as it ground out the ashes of this place were heart-wrenching to see and hear.

Roman collapsed to his knees, shock written over his face. He let his head fall into his hands.

"No one will ever know. They'll never know how close they were to something so wonderful," Roman said. His voice was raw, hard-edged with grief and smoke.

Carmen approached without a word and gripped his shoulder.

None of them had believed this day would ever come, that they'd have to say goodbye to such a bastion of magic and wonder. But there it was, and there it went. And the Manor disappeared into the field with an echoing crash. The earth swallowed it up and the field lost its glamor as the acreage reverted to what it once was.

Hundreds of years ago it was merely a field, bordered by forest. The property slipped back into rolling pasture, untouched by any hands, Guardians or otherwise.

The five remained where they were. They watched the sun set, watched the clouds catch fire, ignited by the sinking of the daylight. They watched as the sky glowed red and eternal over where their home once stood.

The Guardians remained motionless until darkness fell and the moon rose and the sky was washed cleaned of the haze in the air from the flames. And when the stars twinkled and the wind blew with the edge of winter, an icy bitter taste of the months to come, the Guardians finally left.

Epilogue

It had been quiet for an entire week. The Guardians had settled into their new arrangements, in new rooms at the quiet seaside space of the Freemont House.

Carmen enjoyed sitting on the wraparound porch, settled into a rocking chair, wrapped in a cashmere throw. The sound of the sea was a calming ebb and flow. Soon, it would be far too cold to sit outside. The air would fill with the spray and wet of a raging sea from below the cliff walls. The paths and road were already slippery with half-frozen crystals and would only become more treacherous.

Finnigan couldn't be torn from the fireside even when begged. He, instead, practiced slipping in and out of the undercurrent and absorbed the information it provided. He traveled the variations that the Freemont House would eventually begin to shift into and learned as much as he could. The House was becoming more active every day, getting comfortable with its own possibilities.

It was in the little things, at first. An extra closet where once a window brightened the end of a hallway. A portrait that hung over the toilet in the third-floor washroom that couldn't seem to decide who it wanted to be of from day to day. Caden swore that once it had been a dramatically rendered oil painting of a hedgehog, in full military gear.

In what world this was necessary, Caden hoped never to discover. He almost laughed at the sheer number of medals the hedgehog had obtained, but figured it rude. He was clearly a decorated veteran.

Flynn did the best he could to make the Guardians feel safe and at home in a new version of their reality. One in which the Manor no longer existed.

There had been many sleepless nights, many steps wandered through the halls, unsure of where they were. Unsure if they could stay. But Roman had given the all-clear and after they soon lost the haggard confusion that haunted their days.

Flynn had done a fine job of improving the access to the energy of the undercurrent at the Freemont House. It was more than enough for them all to comfortably coexist. The lack of extra rooms, at least for now, until the House began to shift properly, meant an instant excuse to turn humans away. There was nowhere for them to stay at this bed and breakfast. The Guardians did not have to lie to the people they existed to protect.

It was one of these solemn days, when the Freemont House was at its quietest, that a visitor arrived. The Guardians were alone in their spaces and places and had enjoyed the solitude of the House when the doorbell rang. Repeatedly and rapidly, it stirred them all from their hideaways.

Caden and Carmen leaned over the banister of the third floor and stared down at the pattern the stained glass drew along the hardwood. A shadow of a person was outlined in the brilliant blues and reds.

Finnigan popped his head around the kitchen doorway, where he attempted a recipe for blueberry pie, flour smudged on his cheeks and juice staining his hands.

Roman had just hung up his coat in the back of the House. He had spent the last few hours raking around the massive oaks that lined the cliff edge at the rear of the property. His boots were still coated in wet leaves and crumbling mud.

Flynn waved them all away and answered the door, his speech about being fully booked already prepared on the tip of his tongue. But when the door swung open under his hand and he saw the stranger that stood there, something made him pause.

He wasn't sure if it was the desperation in the man's piercing blue eyes or the shadows underneath them. Whether it was the gaunt appearance of his cheeks or how his clothes hung from his bony frame. But something made him throw the door wide and gesture for him to come in.

Maybe it was the way the air almost shimmered when in contact with him, a strange sort of energy that Flynn had to half squint to see. Something about this man, at the very core of him, wasn't quite right.

Wasn't quite *human.*

And it was that otherworldly sheen to him which caused Roman to pause when he entered the hallway to see who Flynn had met at the door. Roman raised a hand toward the sitting room, and wordlessly allowed the stranger to pass in front of him. He gave Flynn a strange look that zipped electric between them.

The man sat, hesitant. He thrummed with a half-hidden anxiety, pressed into the corner of the couch with his gangly limbs thrown about. He looked around the room.

Finnigan and the others drifted into doorways, curious about the silence and the intrusion.

The stranger stared back, glowing pale beneath dark scruff. He looked as if he had recently recovered from an illness or a long period indoors and incapacitated. He pulled off his coat, hands shaking, and clasped his hands together, then raked one hand through his hair. He cleared his throat and his lips trembled, as if he spent every second on the edge of completely becoming lost.

Flynn sat down next to him, body turned toward the stranger and tried to look as encouraging as possible. Something akin to static came off him in waves, and Flynn eyed a few of the loose threads of the afghan on the back of the sofa curve toward him as if attracted to his distress.

When Shadows Creep

The stranger grasped at his own hands, twisted them around, and then rose to leave. He only reached as far as the doorway before Caden stopped him, a gentle hand at his shoulder. "Whatever it is, you're where you need to be. You couldn't have found us otherwise, alright? Just please, go and sit."

The man inhaled deeply and looked at him hard. He seemed to study his face and then study beyond it—more of it— than what his eyes *actually* saw.

Caden inhaled sharply. "You can see us, can't you? I mean, the *real* us," he whispered.

The man nodded, slowly, and lowered his eyes to his feet.

Caden gently turned the man and gave him a small push towards the couch. He seemed to collapse, lifeless, back onto the cushions. The stranger rested his forehead in his hand for a moment then shook his head. He was coming to an internal agreement. He looked up, then, wide-eyed, where Roman stood staring at him.

The stranger pushed his sleeves up. The skin on his arms was distressed and crossed from wrist to elbow with shining and metallic scars. The Guardians stared at these marks and the eerie glow coming off of them, as only seen through their eyes.

Flynn closed his good eye and looked at the man with the other, the one that saw the truth.

"What do you see, Flynn?" Roman asked.

"A glow. Twisting and coursing around him, around his heart like a gilded golden cage." He breathed heavily.

Roman could tell Flynn was not afraid of this man. He didn't, then, have a single scrap of the Dark around him.

"It's the antithesis of everything we've embattled," Flynn said looking back up at Roman.

Roman's heart skipped in his chest. If only this man had shown himself to their door well before they had gone up against the Darkness. They would have won, and easily. Maybe the Manor would not have fallen.

The Freemont House settled and loud cracks came from the aged timbers. They cut through the silence that surrounded them all as they waited, waited for this man to explain why and how he had found them.

And why he had such a profound effect on the reality that surrounded him.

Roman wanted to reach out and touch the bare skin of his arm, to trace the silver lines that ran across in heavy slashes, too numerous to count. They were significant, to whatever this man was. If he could even call him that, a man.

The stranger cleared his throat. "I left others in the car. I didn't... I didn't think it was wise to overwhelm you all. I thought perhaps numbers would intimidate. I didn't want to be sent away."

When Shadows Creep

Roman nodded in acquiescence, and approached where the stranger sat. "That was very kind of you. We don't often get visitors. And certainly none with your unique representation."

The man half choked on a laugh, a wistful sort of smile. "We'd thought it was gone. Thought we were back to normal. But I guess it really never goes away, does it? The supernatural."

Roman tilted his head in response, a half-nod mixed with a shrug. He didn't quite understand.

The man hung his hands between his knees. He looked awkward and young and small. He seemed embarrassed that he'd said something out of turn.

"Not to say I guess, that the supernatural isn't normal... but you know what I mean, right?" He asked.

Finnigan grinned from his spot in the door frame, and shook his head. "If you'd seen what we've been through over the past week or so, we'd have been glad to be normal. No doubt there."

The stranger grinned uneasily and nodded in agreement.

There was far more to the story behind him than he would volunteer. An air of heartache settled over him, heavy as a mantle, a thickness of atmosphere. A loss.

The man watched as a still life painting of a violently red apple paired with a violin faded from existence on the wall. A bowl of exotic fruit appeared out of thin air on a coffee table that flickered through four different colors before it settled on a dappled mossy green.

The stranger stared at the changes with interest rather than fear. This gave Roman the nudge he needed. Whatever this man needed, it must be well within their realm to help him, or the House would have been silent in his presence.

Roman sat down across from him, leaned forward across his knees. "Please, start from the beginning."

The stranger took a deep breath, a quick glance around the room at the Guardians, and then began. "My name is Deacon Masterson, and I have heard that the residents here have experience with traveling between worlds. I need to find someone, need to know if they're still alive, and I've come all the way here because you're my last hope at getting answers."

Roman absorbed the words, studied the man and the pain behind his eyes, and the curious confusion in the others around him.

"Well, Deacon my boy, you've come to the right place. Let's get started, shall we?"

. . .

Until Next Time.

Visit us at:

www.antcolonypress.com

www.facebook.com/antcolonypress

Also by Ant Colony Press

Unconventional by Scarlet Birch

Sam isn't supposed to be in love with Louis. She likes him. What they have is fine. But Love? When he drops the L word, she won't say it back, and she may lose Louis—the only constant thing in her life—forever. He won't give up on her, though, and as her life falls apart he is the foundation she didn't know she needed.

About the Author

Based in Hamilton, Ontario, there's nothing K. likes more than life on the road. Long drives, cheap hotels and gas station snack food, it all adds up to the time of her life. When she's not in a car gathering inspiration for her newest work, she has a long time career in advertising.

9 781940 560472